I0764313

# *An 'Attic' Philosopher*

(Un Philosophe sous les Toits)

# *An 'Attic' Philosopher*

(Un Philosophe sous les Toits)

Émile Souvestre

*With an Introduction By*

Joseph Bertrand

*de l'Académie Française*

ÆGYPAN PRESS

*An 'Attic' Philosopher*
A publication of
ÆGYPAN PRESS
www.aegypan.com

# Émile Souvestre

No one succeeds in obtaining a prominent place in literature, or in surrounding himself with a faithful and steady circle of admirers drawn from the fickle masses of the public, unless he possesses originality, constant variety, and a distinct personality. It is quite possible to gain for a moment a few readers by imitating some original feature in another; but these soon vanish and the writer remains alone and forgotten. Others, again, without belonging to any distinct group of authors, having found their standard in themselves, moralists and educators at the same time, have obtained undying recognition.

Of the latter class, though little known outside of France, is Émile Souvestre, who was born in Morlaix, April 15, 1806, and died at Paris July 5, 1854. He was the son of a civil engineer, was educated at the college of Pontivy, and intended to follow his father's career by entering the Polytechnic School. His father, however, died in 1823, and Souvestre matriculated as a law-student at Rennes. But the young student soon devoted himself entirely to literature. His first essay, a tragedy, *Le Siege de Missolonghi* (1828), was a pronounced failure. Disheartened and disgusted he left Paris and established himself first as a lawyer in Morlaix. Then he became proprietor of a newspaper, and was afterward appointed a professor in Brest and in Mulhouse. In 1836 he contributed to the *Revue des Deux Mondes* some sketches of life in Brittany, which obtained a brilliant success. Souvestre was soon made editor of La Revue de Paris, and in consequence early found a publisher for his first novel, *L'Echelle de Femmes,* which, as was the case with his second work, *Riche et Pauvre,* met with a very favorable reception. His reputation was now made, and between this period and his death he gave to France about sixty volumes – tales, novels, essays, history, and drama.

A double purpose was always very conspicuous in his books: he aspired to the role of a moralist and educator, and was likewise a most impressive painter of the life, character, and morals of the inhabitants of Brittany.

The most significant of his books are perhaps *Les Derniers Bretons* (1835–1837, 4 vols.), *Pierre Landais* (1843, 2 vols.), *Le Foyer Breton* (1844, 2 vols.), *Un Philosophe sons les Toits,* crowned by the Academy (1850), *Confessions d'un Ouvrier* (1851), *Recits et Souvenirs* (1853), *Souvenirs d'un Vieillard* (1854); also *La Bretagne Pittoresque* (1845), and, finally, *Causeries Historiques et Litteraires* (1854, 2 vols.). His comedies deserve honorable mention: *Henri Hamelin, L'Oncle Baptiste* (1842), *La Parisienne, Le Mousse,* etc. In 1848, Souvestre was appointed professor of the newly created school of administration, mostly devoted to popular lectures. He held this post till 1853, lecturing partly in Paris, partly in Switzerland.

His death, when comparatively young, left a distinct gap in the literary world. A life like his could not be extinguished without general sorrow. Although he was unduly modest, and never aspired to the role of a beacon-light in literature, always seeking to remain in obscurity, the works of Émile Souvestre must be placed in the first rank by their morality and by their instructive character. They will always command the entire respect and applause of mankind. And thus it happens that, like many others, he was only fully appreciated after his death.

Even those of his *confrères* who did not seem to esteem him, when alive, suddenly found out that they had experienced a great loss in his demise. They expressed it in emotional panegyrics; contemporaneous literature discovered that virtue had flown from its bosom, and the French Academy, which had at its proper time crowned his *Philosophe sons les Toits* as a work contributing supremely to morals, kept his memory green by bestowing on his widow the "Prix Lambert," designed for the "families of authors who by their integrity, and by the probity of their efforts have well deserved this token from the Republique des Lettres."

Joseph Bertrand
*de l'Académie Française*

# *Chapter I*

## NEW YEAR'S GIFTS

January 1st

The day of the month came into my mind as soon as I awoke. Another year is separated from the chain of ages, and drops into the gulf of the past! The crowd hasten to welcome her young sister. But while all looks are turned toward the future, mine revert to the past. Everyone smiles upon the new queen; but, in spite of myself, I think of her whom time has just wrapped in her winding-sheet. The past year! – at least I know what she was, and what she has given me; while this one comes surrounded by all the forebodings of the unknown. What does she hide in the clouds that mantle her? Is it the storm or the sunshine? Just now it rains, and I feel my mind as gloomy as the sky. I have a holiday today; but what can one do on a rainy day? I walk up and down my attic out of temper, and I determine to light my fire.

Unfortunately the matches are bad, the chimney smokes, the wood goes out! I throw down my bellows in disgust, and sink into my old armchair.

In truth, why should I rejoice to see the birth of a new year? All those who are already in the streets, with holiday looks and smiling faces – do they understand what makes them so gay? Do they even know what is the meaning of this holiday, or whence comes the custom of New Year's gifts?

Here my mind pauses to prove to itself its superiority over that of the vulgar. I make a parenthesis in my ill-temper in favor of my vanity, and I bring together all the evidence which my knowledge can produce.

(The old Romans divided the year into ten months only; it was Numa Pompilius who added January and February. The former took its name from Janus, to whom it was dedicated. As it opened the new year, they surrounded its beginning with good omens, and thence came the custom of visits between neighbors, of wishing happiness, and of New Year's gifts. The presents given by the Romans were symbolic. They consisted of dry figs, dates, honeycomb, as emblems of "the sweetness of the auspices under which the year should begin its course," and a small piece of money called stips, which foreboded riches.)

Here I close the parenthesis, and return to my ill-humor. The little speech I have just addressed to myself has restored me my self-satisfaction, but made me more dissatisfied with others. I could now enjoy my breakfast; but the portress has forgotten my morning's milk, and the pot of preserves is empty! Anyone else would have been vexed: as for me, I affect the most supreme indifference. There remains a hard crust, which I break by main strength, and which I carelessly nibble, as a man far above the vanities of the world and of fresh rolls.

However, I do not know why my thoughts should grow more gloomy by reason of the difficulties of mastication. I once read the story of an Englishman who hanged himself because they had brought him his tea without sugar. There are hours in life when the most trifling cross takes the form of a calamity. Our tempers are like an opera-glass, which makes the object small or great according to the end you look through.

Usually, the prospect that opens out before my window delights me. It is a mountain-range of roofs, with ridges crossing, interlacing, and piled on one another, and upon which tall chimneys raise their peaks. It was but yesterday that they had an Alpine aspect to me, and I waited for the first snowstorm to see glaciers among them; today, I only see tiles and stone flues. The pigeons, which assisted my rural illusions, seem no more than miserable birds which have mistaken the roof for the back yard; the smoke, which rises in light clouds, instead of making me dream of the panting of Vesuvius, reminds me of kitchen preparations and dishwater; and lastly, the telegraph, that I see far off on the old tower of Montmartre, has the effect of a vile gallows stretching its arms over the city.

My eyes, thus hurt by all they meet, fall upon the great man's house which faces my attic.

The influence of New Year's Day is visible there. The servants have an air of eagerness proportioned to the value of their New Year's gifts, received or expected. I see the master of the house crossing the court with the morose look of a man who is forced to be generous; and the visitors increase, followed by shop porters who carry flowers, bandboxes, or toys. Suddenly the great gates are opened, and a new carriage, drawn by thoroughbred horses, draws up before the doorsteps. They are, without doubt, the New Year's gift presented to the mistress of the house by her husband; for she comes herself to look at the new equipage. Very soon she gets into it with a little girl, all streaming with laces, feathers and velvets, and loaded with parcels which she goes to distribute as New Year's gifts. The door is shut, the windows are drawn up, the carriage sets off.

Thus all the world are exchanging good wishes and presents today. I alone have nothing to give or to receive. Poor Solitary! I do not even know one chosen being for whom I might offer a prayer.

Then let my wishes for a happy New Year go and seek out all my unknown friends – lost in the multitude which murmurs like the ocean at my feet!

To you first, hermits in cities, for whom death and poverty have created a solitude in the midst of the crowd! unhappy laborers, who are condemned to toil in melancholy, and eat your daily bread in silence and desertion, and whom God has withdrawn from the intoxicating pangs of love and friendship!

To you, fond dreamers, who pass through life with your eyes turned toward some polar star, while you tread with indifference over the rich harvests of reality!

To you, honest fathers, who lengthen out the evening to maintain your families! to you, poor widows, weeping and working by a cradle! to you, young men, resolutely set to open for yourselves a path in life, large enough to lead through it the wife of your choice! to you, all brave soldiers of work and of self-sacrifice!

To you, lastly, whatever your title and your name, who love good, who pity the suffering; who walk through the world like the symbolical Virgin of Byzantium, with both arms open to the human race!

Here I am suddenly interrupted by loud and increasing chirpings. I look about me: my window is surrounded with sparrows picking up the crumbs of bread which in my brown study I had just scattered on the roof. At this sight a flash of light broke upon my saddened heart. I deceived myself just now, when I complained that I had nothing to give: thanks to me, the sparrows of this part of the town will have their New Year's gifts!

Twelve o'clock. – A knock at my door; a poor girl comes in, and greets me by name. At first I do not recollect her; but she looks at me, and smiles. Ah! it is Paulette! But it is almost a year since I have seen her, and Paulette is no longer the same: the other day she was a child, now she is almost a young woman.

Paulette is thin, pale, and miserably clad; but she has always the same open and straightforward look – the same mouth, smiling at every word, as if to court your sympathy – the same voice, somewhat timid, yet expressing fondness. Paulette is not pretty – she is even thought plain;

as for me, I think her charming. Perhaps that is not on her account, but on my own. Paulette appears to me as one of my happiest recollections.

It was the evening of a public holiday. Our principal buildings were illuminated with festoons of fire, a thousand flags waved in the night winds, and the fireworks had just shot forth their spouts of flame into the midst of the Champ de Mars. Suddenly, one of those unaccountable alarms which strike a multitude with panic fell upon the dense crowd: they cry out, they rush on headlong; the weaker ones fall, and the frightened crowd tramples them down in its convulsive struggles. I escaped from the confusion by a miracle, and was hastening away, when the cries of a perishing child arrested me: I reentered that human chaos, and, after unheard-of exertions, I brought Paulette out of it at the peril of my life.

That was two years ago: since then I had not seen the child again but at long intervals, and I had almost forgotten her; but Paulette's memory was that of a grateful heart, and she came at the beginning of the year to offer me her wishes for my happiness. She brought me, besides, a wallflower in full bloom; she herself had planted and reared it: it was something that belonged wholly to herself; for it was by her care, her perseverance, and her patience, that she had obtained it.

The wallflower had grown in a common pot; but Paulette, who is a bandbox-maker, had put it into a case of varnished paper, ornamented with arabesques. These might have been in better taste, but I did not feel the attention and good-will the less.

This unexpected present, the little girl's modest blushes, the compliments she stammered out, dispelled, as by a sunbeam, the kind of mist which had gathered round my mind; my thoughts suddenly changed from the leaden tints of evening to the brightest colors of dawn. I made Paulette sit down, and questioned her with a light heart.

At first the little girl replied in monosyllables; but very soon the tables were turned, and it was I who interrupted with short interjections her long and confidential talk. The poor child leads a hard life. She was left an orphan long since, with a brother and sister, and lives with an old grandmother, who has "brought them up to poverty," as she always calls it.

However, Paulette now helps her to make bandboxes, her little sister Perrine begins to use the needle, and her brother Henry is apprentice to a printer. All would go well if it were not for losses and want of work – if it were not for clothes which wear out, for appetites which grow larger, and for the winter, when you cannot get sunshine for nothing. Paulette complains that her candles go too quickly, and that her wood costs too much. The fireplace in their garret is so large that a fagot makes no more show in it than a match; it is so near the roof that the wind blows the rain down it, and in winter it hails upon the hearth; so they have left off using it. Henceforth they must be content with an earthen chafing-dish, upon which they cook their meals. The grandmother had often spoken of a stove that was for sale at the broker's close by; but he asked seven francs for it, and the times are too hard for such an expense: the family, therefore, resign themselves to cold for economy!

As Paulette spoke, I felt more and more that I was losing my fretfulness and low spirits. The first disclosures of the little bandbox-maker created within me a wish that soon became a plan. I questioned her about her daily occupations, and she informed me that on leaving me she must go, with her brother, her sister, and grandmother, to the different people for whom they work. My plan was immediately settled. I told the child that I would go to see her in the evening, and I sent her away with fresh thanks.

I placed the wallflower in the open window, where a ray of sunshine bid it welcome; the birds were singing around, the sky had cleared up, and the day, which began so loweringly, had become bright. I sang as I moved about my room, and, having hastily put on my hat and coat, I went out.

Three o'clock. – All is settled with my neighbor, the chimney-doctor; he will repair my old stove, and answers for its being as good as new. At five o'clock we are to set out, and put it up in Paulette's grandmother's room.

Midnight. – All has gone off well. At the hour agreed upon, I was at the old bandbox-maker's; she was still out. My Piedmontese* fixed the stove, while I arranged a dozen logs in the great fireplace, taken from my winter stock. I shall make up for them by warming myself with walking, or by going to bed earlier.

My heart beat at every step that was heard on the staircase; I trembled lest they should interrupt me in my preparations, and should thus spoil my intended surprise. But no! – see everything ready: the lighted stove murmurs gently, the little lamp burns upon the table, and a bottle of oil for it is provided on the shelf. The chimney-doctor is gone. Now my fear lest they should come is changed into impatience at their not coming. At last I hear children's voices; here they are: they push open the door and rush in – but they all stop in astonishment.

At the sight of the lamp, the stove, and the visitor, who stands there like a magician in the midst of these wonders, they draw back almost frightened. Paulette is the first to comprehend it, and the arrival of the

* In Paris a chimney-sweeper is named "Piedmontese" or "Savoyard," as they usually come from that country.

grandmother, who is more slowly mounting the stairs, finishes the explanation. Then come tears, ecstasies, thanks!

But the wonders are not yet ended. The little sister opens the oven, and discovers some chestnuts just roasted; the grandmother puts her hand on the bottles of cider arranged on the dresser; and I draw forth from the basket that I have hidden a cold tongue, a pot of butter, and some fresh rolls.

Now their wonder turns into admiration; the little family have never seen such a feast! They lay the cloth, they sit down, they eat; it is a complete banquet for all, and each contributes his share to it. I had brought only the supper: and the bandbox-maker and her children supplied the enjoyment.

What bursts of laughter at nothing! What a hubbub of questions which waited for no reply, of replies which answered no question! The old woman herself shared in the wild merriment of the little ones! I have always been struck at the ease with which the poor forget their wretchedness. Being used to live only for the present, they make a gain of every pleasure as soon as it offers itself. But the surfeited rich are more difficult to satisfy: they require time and everything to suit before they will consent to be happy.

The evening has passed like a moment. The old woman told me the history of her life, sometimes smiling, sometimes drying her eyes. Perrine sang an old ballad with her fresh young voice. Henry told us what he knows of the great writers of the day, to whom he has to carry their proofs. At last we were obliged to separate, not without fresh thanks on the part of the happy family.

I have come home slowly, ruminating with a full heart, and pure enjoyment, on the simple events of my evening. It has given me much comfort and much instruction. Now, no New Year's Day will come amiss to me; I know that no one is so unhappy as to have nothing to give and nothing to receive.

As I came in, I met my rich neighbor's new equipage. She, too, had just returned from her evening's party; and, as she sprang from the carriage-step with feverish impatience, I heard her murmur "At last!"

I, when I left Paulette's family, said "So soon!"

# *Chapter II*

## THE CARNIVAL

February 20th

What a noise out of doors! What is the meaning of these shouts and cries? Ah! I recollect: this is the last day of the Carnival, and the maskers are passing.

Christianity has not been able to abolish the noisy bacchanalian festivals of the pagan times, but it has changed the names. That which it has given to these "days of liberty" announces the ending of the feasts, and the month of fasting which should follow; carn-ival means, literally, "farewell to flesh!" It is a forty days' farewell to the "blessed pullets and fat hams," so celebrated by Pantagruel's minstrel. Man prepares for privation by satiety, and finishes his sin thoroughly before he begins to repent.

Why, in all ages and among every people, do we meet with someone of these mad festivals? Must we believe that it requires such an effort for men to be reasonable, that the weaker ones have need of rest at intervals? The monks of La Trappe, who are condemned to silence by their rule, are allowed to speak once in a month, and on this day they all talk at once from the rising to the setting of the sun.

Perhaps it is the same in the world. As we are obliged all the year to be decent, orderly, and reasonable, we make up for such a long restraint during the Carnival. It is a door opened to the incongruous fancies and wishes that have hitherto been crowded back into a corner of our brain. For a moment the slaves become the masters, as in the days of the Saturnalia, and all is given up to the "fools of the family."

The shouts in the square redouble; the troops of masks increase – on foot, in carriages, and on horseback. It is now who can attract the most attention by making a figure for a few hours, or by exciting curiosity or envy; tomorrow they will all return, dull and exhausted, to the employments and troubles of yesterday.

Alas! thought I with vexation, each of us is like these masqueraders; our whole life is often but an unsightly Carnival! And yet man has need of holidays, to relax his mind, rest his body, and open his heart. Can he not have them, then, with these coarse pleasures? Economists have been long inquiring what is the best disposal of the industry of the human race. Ah! if I could only discover the best disposal of its leisure! It is easy enough to find it work; but who will find it relaxation? Work supplies the daily bread; but it is cheerfulness that gives it a relish. O philosophers! go in quest of pleasure! find us amusements without brutality, enjoyments without selfishness; in a word, invent a Carnival that will please everybody, and bring shame to no one.

Three o'clock. – I have just shut my window, and stirred up my fire. As this is a holiday for everybody, I will make it one for myself, too. So I light the little lamp over which, on grand occasions, I make a cup of the coffee that my portress's son brought from the Levant, and I look in my bookcase for one of my favorite authors.

First, here is the amusing parson of Meudon; but his characters are too fond of talking slang: – Voltaire; but he disheartens men by always bantering them: – Molière; but he hinders one's laughter by making one think: – Lesage; let us stop at him. Being profound rather than grave, he preaches virtue while ridiculing vice; if bitterness is sometimes to be found in his writings, it is always in the garb of mirth: he sees the miseries of the world without despising it, and knows its cowardly tricks without hating it.

Let us call up all the heroes of his book. . . . Gil Blas, Fabrice, Sangrado, the Archbishop of Granada, the Duke of Lerma, Aurora, Scipio! Ye gay or graceful figures, rise before my eyes, people my solitude; bring hither for my amusement the world-carnival, of which you are the brilliant maskers!

Unfortunately, at the very moment I made this invocation, I recollected I had a letter to write which could not be put off. One of my attic neighbors came yesterday to ask me to do it. He is a cheerful old man, and has a passion for pictures and prints. He comes home almost every day with a drawing or painting – probably of little value; for I know he lives penuriously, and even the letter that I am to write for him shows his poverty. His only son, who was married in England, is just dead, and his widow – left without any means, and with an old mother and a child – had written to beg for a home. M. Antoine asked me first to translate the letter, and then to write a refusal. I had promised that he should have this answer today: before everything, let us fulfill our promises.

The sheet of "Bath" paper is before me, I have dipped my pen into the ink, and I rub my forehead to invite forth a sally of ideas, when I perceive that I have not my dictionary. Now, a Parisian who would speak English without a dictionary is like a child without leading-strings; the ground trembles under him, and he stumbles at the first step. I run then to the bookbinder's, where I left my Johnson, who lives close by in the square.

The door is half open; I hear low groans; I enter without knocking, and I see the bookbinder by the bedside of his fellow-lodger. This latter has a violent fever and delirium. Pierre looks at him perplexed and out of humor. I learn from him that his comrade was not able to get up in the morning, and that since then he has become worse every hour.

I ask whether they have sent for a doctor.

"Oh, yes, indeed!" replied Pierre, roughly; "one must have money in one's pocket for that, and this fellow has only debts instead of savings."

"But you," said I, rather astonished; "are you not his friend?"

"Friend!" interrupted the bookbinder. "Yes, as much as the shaft-horse is friend to the leader – on condition that each will take his share of the draft, and eat his feed by himself."

"You do not intend, however, to leave him without any help?"

"Bah! he may keep in his bed till tomorrow, as I'm going to the ball."

"You mean to leave him alone?"

"Well! must I miss a party of pleasure at Courtville* because this fellow is lightheaded?" asked Pierre, sharply. "I have promised to meet some friends at old Desnoyer's. Those who are sick may take their broth; my physic is white wine."

So saying, he untied a bundle, out of which he took the fancy costume of a waterman, and proceeded to dress himself in it.

In vain I tried to awaken some fellow-feeling for the unfortunate man who lay groaning there close by him; being entirely taken up with the thoughts of his expected pleasure, Pierre would hardly so much as hear me. At last his coarse selfishness provoked me. I began reproaching instead of remonstrating with him, and I declared him responsible for the consequences which such a desertion must bring upon the sick man.

At this the bookbinder, who was just going, stopped with an oath, and stamped his foot. "Am I to spend my Carnival in heating water for footbaths, pray?"

"You must not leave your comrade to die without help!" I replied.

"Let him go to the hospital, then!"

"How can he by himself?"

* A Parisian summer resort.

Pierre seemed to make up his mind.

"Well, I'm going to take him," resumed he; "besides, I shall get rid of him sooner. Come, get up, comrade!" He shook his comrade, who had not taken off his clothes. I observed that he was too weak to walk, but the bookbinder would not listen: he made him get up, and half dragged, half supported him to the lodge of the porter, who ran for a hackney carriage. I saw the sick man get into it, almost fainting, with the impatient waterman; and they both set off, one perhaps to die, the other to dine at Courtville Gardens!

Six o'clock. – I have been to knock at my neighbor's door, who opened it himself; and I have given him his letter, finished at last, and directed to his son's widow. M. Antoine thanked me gratefully, and made me sit down.

It was the first time I had been into the attic of the old amateur. Curtains stained with damp and hanging down in rags, a cold stove, a bed of straw, two broken chairs, composed all the furniture. At the end of the room were a great number of prints in a heap, and paintings without frames turned against the wall.

At the moment I came in, the old man was making his dinner on some hard crusts of bread, which he was soaking in a glass of *eau sucree.* He perceived that my eyes fell upon his hermit fare, and he looked a little ashamed.

"There is nothing to tempt you in my supper, neighbor," said he, with a smile.

I replied that at least I thought it a very philosophical one for the Carnival.

M. Antoine shook his head, and went on again with his supper.

"Everyone keeps his holidays in his own way," resumed he, beginning again to dip a crust into his glass. "There are several sorts of epicures, and not all feasts are meant to regale the palate; there are some also for the ears and the eyes."

I looked involuntarily round me, as if to seek for the invisible banquet which could make up to him for such a supper.

Without doubt he understood me; for he got up slowly, and, with the magisterial air of a man confident in what he is about to do, he rummaged behind several picture frames, drew forth a painting, over which he passed his hand, and silently placed it under the light of the lamp.

It represented a fine-looking old man, seated at table with his wife, his daughter, and his children, and singing to the accompaniment of musicians who appeared in the background. At first sight I recognized the subject, which I had often admired at the Louvre, and I declared it to be a splendid copy of Jordaens.

"A copy!" cried M. Antoine; "say an original, neighbor, and an original retouched by Rubens! Look closer at the head of the old man, the dress of the young woman, and the accessories. One can count the pencil-strokes of the Hercules of painters. It is not only a masterpiece, sir; it is a treasure – a relic! The picture at the Louvre may be a pearl, this is a diamond!"

And resting it against the stove, so as to place it in the best light, he fell again to soaking his crusts, without taking his eyes off the wonderful picture. One would have said that the sight of it gave the crusts an unexpected relish, for he chewed them slowly, and emptied his glass by little sips. His shriveled features became smooth, his nostrils expanded; it was indeed, as he said himself, "a feast for the eyes."

"You see that I also have my treat," he resumed, nodding his head with an air of triumph. "Others may run after dinners and balls; as for me, this is the pleasure I give myself for my Carnival."

"But if this painting is really so precious," replied I, "it ought to be worth a high price."

"Eh! eh!" said M. Antoine, with an air of proud indifference. "In good times, a good judge might value it at somewhere about twenty thousand francs."

I started back.

"And you have bought it?" cried I.

"For nothing," replied he, lowering his voice. "These brokers are asses; mine mistook this for a student's copy; he let me have it for fifty louis, ready money! This morning I took them to him, and now he wishes to be off the bargain."

"This morning!" repeated I, involuntarily casting my eyes on the letter containing the refusal that M. Antoine had made me write to his son's widow, which was still on the little table.

He took no notice of my exclamation, and went on contemplating the work of Jordaens in an ecstasy.

"What a knowledge of chiaroscuro!" he murmured, biting his last crust in delight. "What relief! what fire! Where can one find such transparency of color! such magical lights! such force! such nature!"

As I was listening to him in silence, he mistook my astonishment for admiration, and clapped me on the shoulder.

"You are dazzled," said he merrily; "you did not expect such a treasure! What do you say to the bargain I have made?"

"Pardon me," replied I, gravely; "but I think you might have done better."

M. Antoine raised his head.

"How!" cried he; "do you take me for a man likely to be deceived about the merit or value of a painting?"

"I neither doubt your taste nor your skill; but I cannot help thinking that, for the price of this picture of a family party, you might have had –"

"What then?"

"The family itself, sir."

The old amateur cast a look at me, not of anger, but of contempt. In his eyes I had evidently just proved myself a barbarian, incapable of understanding the arts, and unworthy of enjoying them. He got up without answering me, hastily took up the Jordaens, and replaced it in its hiding place behind the prints.

It was a sort of dismissal; I took leave of him, and went away.

Seven o'clock. – When I come in again, I find my water boiling over my lamp, and I busy myself in grinding my Mocha, and setting out my coffee-things.

The getting coffee ready is the most delicate and most attractive of domestic operations to one who lives alone: it is the grand work of a bachelor's housekeeping.

Coffee is, so to say, just the mid-point between bodily and spiritual nourishment. It acts agreeably, and at the same time, upon the senses and the thoughts. Its very fragrance gives a sort of delightful activity to the wits; it is a genius that lends wings to our fancy, and transports it to the land of the Arabian Nights.

When I am buried in my old easy chair, my feet on the fender before a blazing fire, my ear soothed by the singing of the coffee-pot, which seems to gossip with my fire-irons, the sense of smell gently excited by the aroma of the Arabian bean, and my eyes shaded by my cap pulled down over them, it often seems as if each cloud of the fragrant steam took a distinct form. As in the mirages of the desert, in each as it rises, I see some image of which my mind had been longing for the reality.

At first the vapor increases, and its color deepens. I see a cottage on a hillside: behind is a garden shut in by a whitethorn hedge, and through the garden runs a brook, on the banks of which I hear the bees humming.

Then the view opens still more. See those fields planted with apple trees, in which I can distinguish a plow and horses waiting for their master! Farther on, in a part of the wood which rings with the sound of the axe, I perceive the woodsman's hut, roofed with turf and branches; and, in the midst of all these rural pictures, I seem to see a figure of myself gliding about. It is my ghost walking in my dream!

The bubbling of the water, ready to boil over, compels me to break off my meditations, in order to fill up the coffee-pot. I then remember that I have no cream; I take my tin can off the hook and go down to the milkwoman's.

Mother Denis is a hale countrywoman from Savoy, which she left when quite young; and, contrary to the custom of the Savoyards, she has not gone back to it again. She has neither husband nor child, notwithstanding the title they give her; but her kindness, which never sleeps, makes her worthy of the name of mother.

A brave creature! Left by herself in the battle of life, she makes good her humble place in it by working, singing, helping others, and leaving the rest to God.

At the door of the milk-shop I hear loud bursts of laughter. In one of the corners of the shop three children are sitting on the ground. They wear the sooty dress of Savoyard boys, and in their hands they hold large slices of bread and cheese. The youngest is besmeared up to the eyes with his, and that is the reason of their mirth.

Mother Denis points them out to me.

"Look at the little lambs, how they enjoy themselves!" said she, putting her hand on the head of the little glutton.

"He has had no breakfast," puts in one of the others by way of excuse.

"Poor little thing," said the milkwoman; "he is left alone in the streets of Paris, where he can find no other father than the All-good God!"

"And that is why you make yourself a mother to them?" I replied, gently.

"What I do is little enough," said Mother Denis, measuring out my milk; "but every day I get some of them together out of the street, that for once they may have enough to eat. Dear children! their mothers will make up for it in heaven. Not to mention that they recall my native mountains to me: when they sing and dance, I seem to see our old father again."

Here her eyes filled with tears.

"So you are repaid by your recollections for the good you do them?" resumed I.

"Yes! yes!" said she, "and by their happiness, too! The laughter of these little ones, sir, is like a bird's song; it makes you gay, and gives you heart to live."

As she spoke she cut some fresh slices of bread and cheese, and added some apples and a handful of nuts to them.

"Come, my little dears," she cried, "put these into your pockets against tomorrow."

Then, turning to me:

"Today I am ruining myself," added she; "but we must all have our Carnival."

I came away without saying a word: I was too much affected.

At last I have discovered what true pleasure is. After beholding the egotism of sensuality and of intellect, I have found the happy self-sacrifice of goodness. Pierre, M. Antoine, and Mother Denis had all kept their Carnival; but for the first two, it was only a feast for the senses or the mind; while for the third, it was a feast for the heart.

# Chapter III

## WHAT WE MAY LEARN BY LOOKING OUT OF WINDOW

March 3d

A poet has said that life is the dream of a shadow: he would better have compared it to a night of fever! What alternate fits of restlessness and sleep! what discomfort! what sudden starts! what ever-returning thirst! what a chaos of mournful and confused fancies! We can neither sleep nor wake; we seek in vain for repose, and we stop short on the brink of action. Two thirds of human existence are wasted in hesitation, and the last third in repenting.

When I say human existence, I mean my own! We are so made that each of us regards himself as the mirror of the community: what passes in our minds infallibly seems to us a history of the universe. Every man is like the drunkard who reports an earthquake, because he feels himself staggering.

And why am I uncertain and restless – I, a poor day-laborer in the world – who fill an obscure station in a corner of it, and whose work it avails itself of, without heeding the workman? I will tell you, my unseen friend, for whom these lines are written; my unknown brother, on whom the solitary call in sorrow; my imaginary confidant, to whom all monologues are addressed and who is but the shadow of our own conscience.

A great event has happened in my life! A crossroad has suddenly opened in the middle of the monotonous way along which I was traveling quietly, and without thinking of it. Two roads present themselves, and I must choose between them. One is only the continuation of that I have followed till now; the other is wider, and exhibits wondrous prospects. On the first there is nothing to fear, but also little to hope; on the other are great dangers and great fortune. Briefly, the question is, whether I shall give up the humble office in which I thought to die, for one of those bold speculations in which chance alone is banker! Ever since yesterday I have consulted with myself; I have compared the two and I remain undecided.

Where shall I find light – who will advise me?

Sunday, 4th. – See the sun coming out from the thick fogs of winter! Spring announces its approach; a soft breeze skims over the roofs, and my wallflower begins to blow again.

We are near that sweet season of fresh green, of which the poets of the sixteenth century sang with so much feeling:

Now the gladsome month of May
All things newly doth array;
Fairest lady, let me too
In thy love my life renew.

The chirping of the sparrows calls me: they claim the crumbs I scatter to them every morning. I open my window, and the prospect of roofs opens out before me in all its splendor.

He who has lived only on a first floor has no idea of the picturesque variety of such a view. He has never contemplated these tile-colored heights which intersect each other; he has not followed with his eyes these gutter-valleys, where the fresh verdure of the attic gardens waves, the deep shadows which evening spreads over the slated slopes, and the sparkling of windows which the setting sun has kindled to a blaze of fire. He has not studied the flora of these Alps of civilization, carpeted by lichens and mosses; he is not acquainted with the myriad inhabitants that people them, from the microscopic insect to the domestic cat – that reynard of the roofs who is always on the prowl, or in ambush; he has not witnessed the thousand aspects of a clear or a cloudy sky; nor the thousand effects of light, that make these upper regions a theater with ever-changing scenes! How many times have my days of leisure passed away in contemplating this wonderful sight; in discovering its darker or brighter episodes; in seeking, in short, in this unknown world for the impressions of travel that wealthy tourists look for lower!

Nine o'clock. – But why, then, have not my winged neighbors picked up the crumbs I have scattered for them before my window? I see them fly away, come back, perch upon the ledges of the windows, and chirp at the sight of the feast they are usually so ready to devour! It is not my presence that frightens them; I have accustomed them to eat out of my hand. Then, why this fearful suspense? In vain I look around: the roof is clear, the windows near are closed. I crumble the bread that remains from my breakfast to attract them by an ampler feast. Their chirpings increase, they bend down their heads, the boldest approach upon the wing, but without daring to alight.

Come, come, my sparrows are the victims of one of the foolish panics which make the funds fall at the Bourse! It is plain that birds are not more reasonable than men!

With this reflection I was about to shut my window, when suddenly I perceived, in a spot of sunshine on my right, the shadow of two pricked-up ears; then a paw advanced, then the head of a tabby-cat showed itself at the corner of the gutter. The cunning fellow was lying there in wait, hoping the crumbs would bring him some game.

And I had accused my guests of cowardice! I was so sure that no danger could menace them! I thought I had looked well everywhere! I had only forgotten the corner behind me!

In life, as on the roofs, how many misfortunes come from having forgotten a single corner!

Ten o'clock. – I cannot leave my window; the rain and the cold have kept it shut so long that I must reconnoiter all the environs to be able to take possession of them again. My eyes search in succession all the points of the jumbled and confused prospect, passing on or stopping according to what they light upon.

Ah! see the windows upon which they formerly loved to rest; they are those of two unknown neighbors, whose different habits they have long remarked.

One is a poor work-woman, who rises before sunrise, and whose profile is shadowed upon her little muslin window-curtain far into the evening; the other is a young songstress, whose vocal flourishes sometimes reach my attic by snatches. When their windows are open, that of the work-woman discovers a humble but decent abode; the other, an elegantly furnished room. But today a crowd of tradespeople throng the latter: they take down the silk hangings and carry off the furniture, and I now remember that the young singer passed under my window this morning with her veil down, and walking with the hasty step of one who suffers some inward trouble. Ah! I guess it all. Her means are exhausted in elegant fancies, or have been taken away by some unexpected misfortune, and now she has fallen from luxury to indigence. While the work-woman manages not only to keep her little room, but also to furnish it with decent comfort by her steady toil, that of the singer is become the property of brokers. The one sparkled for a moment on the wave of prosperity; the other sails slowly but safely along the coast of a humble and laborious industry.

Alas! is there not here a lesson for us all? Is it really in hazardous experiments, at the end of which we shall meet with wealth or ruin, that the wise man should employ his years of strength and freedom? Ought he to consider life as a regular employment which brings its daily wages, or as a game in which the future is determined by a few throws? Why seek the risk of extreme chances? For what end hasten to riches by dangerous roads? Is it really certain that happiness is the prize of brilliant successes, rather than of a wisely accepted poverty? Ah! if men but knew in what a small dwelling joy can live, and how little it costs to furnish it!

Twelve o'clock. – I have been walking up and down my attic for a long time, with my arms folded and my eyes on the ground! My doubts increase, like shadows encroaching more and more on some bright space; my fears multiply; and the uncertainty becomes every moment more painful to me! It is necessary for me to decide today, and before the evening! I hold the dice of my future fate in my hands, and I dare not throw them.

Three o'clock. – The sky has become cloudy, and a cold wind begins to blow from the west; all the windows which were opened to the sunshine of a beautiful day are shut again. Only on the opposite side of the street, the lodger on the last story has not yet left his balcony.

One knows him to be a soldier by his regular walk, his grey moustaches, and the ribbon that decorates his buttonhole. Indeed, one might have guessed as much from the care he takes of the little garden which is the ornament of his balcony in mid-air; for there are two things especially loved by all old soldiers – flowers and children. They have been so long, obliged to look upon the earth as a field of battle, and so long cut off from the peaceful pleasures of a quiet lot, that they seem to begin life at an age when others end it. The tastes of their early years, which were arrested by the stern duties of war, suddenly break out again with their white hairs, and are like the savings of youth which they spend again in old age. Besides, they have been condemned to be destroyers for so long that perhaps they feel a secret pleasure in creating, and seeing life spring up again: the beauty of weakness has a grace and an attraction the more for those who have been the agents of unbending force; and the watching over the frail germs of life has all the charms of novelty for these old workmen of death.

Therefore the cold wind has not driven my neighbor from his balcony. He is digging up the earth in his green boxes, and carefully sowing the seeds of the scarlet nasturtium, convolvulus, and sweet-pea. Henceforth he will come every day to watch for their first sprouting, to protect the young shoots from weeds or insects, to arrange the strings for the tendrils to climb on, and carefully to regulate their supply of water and heat!

How much labor to bring in the desired harvest! For that, how many times shall I see him brave cold or heat, wind or sun, as he does today! But then, in the hot summer days, when the blinding dust whirls in clouds through our streets, when the eye, dazzled by the glare of white stucco, knows not where to rest, and the glowing roofs reflect their heat upon us to burning, the old soldier will sit in his arbor and perceive nothing but green leaves and flowers around him, and the breeze will come cool and fresh to him through these perfumed shades. His assiduous care will be rewarded at last.

We must sow the seeds, and tend the growth, if we would enjoy the flower.

Four o'clock. – The clouds that have been gathering in the horizon for a long time are become darker; it thunders loudly, and the rain pours down! Those who are caught in it fly in every direction, some laughing and some crying.

I always find particular amusement in these helter-skelters, caused by a sudden storm. It seems as if each one, when thus taken by surprise, loses the factitious character that the world or habit has given him, and appears in his true colors.

See, for example, that big man with deliberate step, who suddenly forgets his indifference, made to order, and runs like a schoolboy! He is a thrifty city gentleman, who, with all his fashionable airs, is afraid to spoil his hat.

That pretty woman yonder, on the contrary, whose looks are so modest, and whose dress is so elaborate, slackens her pace with the increasing storm. She seems to find pleasure in braving it, and does not think of her velvet cloak spotted by the hail! She is evidently a lioness in sheep's clothing.

Here, a young man, who was passing, stops to catch some of the hailstones in his hand, and examines them. By his quick and businesslike walk just now, you would have taken him for a tax-gatherer on his rounds, when he is a young philosopher, studying the effects of electricity. And those schoolboys who leave their ranks to run after the sudden gusts of a March whirlwind; those girls, just now so demure, but who now fly with bursts of laughter; those national guards, who quit the martial attitude of their days of duty to take refuge under a porch! The storm has caused all these transformations.

See, it increases! The hardiest are obliged to seek shelter. I see everyone rushing toward the shop in front of my window, which a bill announces is to let. It is for the fourth time within a few months. A year ago all the skill of the joiner and the art of the painter were employed in beautifying it, but their works are already destroyed by the leaving of so many tenants; the cornices of the front are disfigured by mud; the arabesques on the doorway are spoiled by bills posted upon them to announce the sale of the effects. The splendid shop has lost some of its embellishments with each change of the tenant. See it now empty, and left open to the passersby. How much does its fate resemble that of so many who, like it, only change their occupation to hasten the faster to ruin!

I am struck by this last reflection: since the morning everything seems to speak to me, and with the same warning tone. Everything says: "Take care! be content with your happy, though humble lot; happiness can be retained only by constancy; do not forsake your old patrons for the protection of those who are unknown!"

Are they the outward objects which speak thus, or does the warning come from within? Is it not I myself who give this language to all that surrounds me? The world is but an instrument, to which we give sound at will. But what does it signify if it teaches us wisdom? The low voice that speaks in our breasts is always a friendly voice, for it tells us what we are, that is to say, what is our capability. Bad conduct results, for the most part, from mistaking our calling. There are so many fools and knaves, because there are so few men who know themselves. The question is not to discover what will suit us, but for what we are suited!

What should I do among these many experienced financial speculators? I am only a poor sparrow, born among the housetops, and should always fear the enemy crouching in the dark corner; I am a prudent workman, and should think of the business of my neighbors who so suddenly disappeared; I am a timid observer, and should call to mind the flowers so slowly raised by the old soldier, or the shop brought to ruin by constant change of masters. Away from me, ye banquets, over which hangs the sword of Damocles! I am a country mouse. Give me my nuts and hollow tree, and I ask nothing besides – except security.

And why this insatiable craving for riches? Does a man drink more when he drinks from a large glass? Whence comes that universal dread of mediocrity, the fruitful mother of peace and liberty? Ah! there is the evil which, above every other, it should be the aim of both public and private education to anticipate! If that were got rid of, what treasons would be spared, what baseness avoided, what a chain of excess and crime would be forever broken! We award the palm to charity, and to self-sacrifice; but, above all, let us award it to moderation, for it is the great social virtue. Even when it does not create the others, it stands instead of them.

Six o'clock. – I have written a letter of thanks to the promoters of the new speculation, and have declined their offer! This decision has restored my peace of mind. I stopped singing, like the cobbler, as long as I entertained the hope of riches: it is gone, and happiness is come back!

O beloved and gentle Poverty! pardon me for having for a moment wished to fly from thee, as I would from Want. Stay here forever with thy charming sisters, Pity, Patience, Sobriety, and Solitude; be ye my queens and my instructors; teach me the stern duties of life; remove far from my abode the weakness of heart and giddiness of head which follow prosperity. Holy Poverty! teach me to endure without complaining, to impart without grudging, to seek the end of life higher than in pleasure, farther off than in power. Thou givest the body strength, thou makest the mind more firm; and, thanks to thee, this life, to which the rich attach themselves as to a rock, becomes a bark of which death may cut the cable without awakening all our fears. Continue to sustain me, O thou whom Christ hath called Blessed!

# *Chapter IV*

## LET US LOVE ONE ANOTHER

April 9th

The fine evenings are come back; the trees begin to put forth their shoots; hyacinths, jonquils, violets, and lilacs perfume the baskets of the flower-girls – all the world have begun their walks again on the quays and boulevards. After dinner, I, too, descend from my attic to breathe the evening air.

It is the hour when Paris is seen in all its beauty. During the day the plaster fronts of the houses weary the eye by their monotonous whiteness; heavily laden carts make the streets shake under their huge wheels; the eager crowd, taken up by the one fear of losing a moment from business, cross and jostle one another; the aspect of the city altogether has something harsh, restless, and flurried about it. But, as soon as the stars appear, everything is changed; the glare of the white houses is quenched in the gathering shades; you hear no more any rolling but that of the carriages on their way to some party of pleasure; you see only the lounger or the light-hearted passing by; work has given place to leisure. Now each one may breathe after the fierce race through the business of the day, and whatever strength remains to him he gives to pleasure! See the ballrooms lighted up, the theaters open, the eating-shops along the walks set out with dainties, and the twinkling lanterns of the newspaper criers. Decidedly Paris has laid aside the pen, the ruler, and the apron; after the day spent in work, it must have the evening for enjoyment; like the masters of Thebes, it has put off all serious matter till tomorrow.

I love to take part in this happy hour; not to mix in the general gayety, but to contemplate it. If the enjoyments of others embitter jealous minds, they strengthen the humble spirit; they are the beams of sunshine, which open the two beautiful flowers called trust and hope.

Although alone in the midst of the smiling multitude, I do not feel myself isolated from it, for its gayety is reflected upon me: it is my own kind, my own family, who are enjoying life, and I take a brother's share in their happiness. We are all fellow-soldiers in this earthly battle, and what does it matter on whom the honors of the victory fall? If Fortune passes by without seeing us, and pours her favors on others, let us console ourselves, like the friend of Parmenio, by saying, "Those, too, are Alexanders."

While making these reflections, I was going on as chance took me. I crossed from one pavement to another, I retraced my steps, I stopped before the shops or to read the handbills. How many things there are to learn in the streets of Paris! What a museum it is! Unknown fruits, foreign arms, furniture of old times or other lands, animals of all climates, statues of great men, costumes of distant nations! It is the world seen in samples!

Let us then look at this people, whose knowledge is gained from the shop windows and the tradesman's display of goods. Nothing has been taught them, but they have a rude notion of everything. They have seen pineapples at Chevet's, a palm tree in the Jardin des Plantes, sugar-canes selling on the Pont-Neuf. The Redskins, exhibited in the Valentine Hall, have taught them to mimic the dance of the bison, and to smoke the calumet of peace; they have seen Carter's lions fed; they know the principal national costumes contained in Babin's collection; Goupil's display of prints has placed the tiger-hunts of Africa and the sittings of the English Parliament before their eyes; they have become acquainted with Queen Victoria, the Emperor of Austria, and Kossuth, at the office-door of the Illustrated News. We can certainly instruct them, but not astonish them; for nothing is completely new to them. You may take the Paris ragamuffin through the five quarters of the world, and at every wonder with which you think to surprise him, he will settle the matter with that favorite and conclusive answer of his class – "I know."

But this variety of exhibitions, which makes Paris the fair of the world, does not offer merely a means of instruction to him who walks through it; it is a continual spur for rousing the imagination, a first step of the ladder always set up before us in a vision. When we see them, how many voyages do we take in imagination, what adventures do we dream of, what pictures do we sketch! I never look at that shop near the Chinese baths, with its tapestry hangings of Florida jasmine, and filled with magnolias, without seeing the forest glades of the New World, described by the author of Atala, opening themselves out before me.

Then, when this study of things and this discourse of reason begin to tire you, look around you! What contrasts of figures and faces you see in the crowd! What a vast field for the exercise of meditation! A half-seen glance, or a few words caught as the speaker passes by, open a thousand vistas to your imagination. You wish to comprehend what these imperfect disclosures mean, and, as the antiquary endeavors to decipher the mutilated inscription on some old monument, you build up a history on a gesture or on a word! These are the stirring sports of the mind, which finds in fiction a relief from the wearisome dullness of the actual.

Alas! as I was just now passing by the carriage-entrance of a great house, I noticed a sad subject for one of these histories. A man was sitting in the darkest corner, with his head bare, and holding out his hat for the charity of those who passed. His threadbare coat had that look of neatness which marks that destitution has been met by a long struggle. He had carefully buttoned it up to hide the want of a shirt. His face was half hid under his grey hair, and his eyes were closed, as if he wished to escape the sight of his own humiliation, and he remained mute and motionless. Those who passed him took no notice of the beggar, who sat in silence and darkness! They had been so lucky as to escape complaints and importunities, and were glad to turn away their eyes too.

Suddenly the great gate turned on its hinges; and a very low carriage, lighted with silver lamps and drawn by two black horses, came slowly out, and took the road toward the Faubourg St. Germain. I could just distinguish, within, the sparkling diamonds and the flowers of a ball-dress; the glare of the lamps passed like a bloody streak over the pale face of the beggar, and showed his look as his eyes opened and followed the rich man's equipage until it disappeared in the night.

I dropped a small piece of money into the hat he was holding out, and passed on quickly.

I had just fallen unexpectedly upon the two saddest secrets of the disease which troubles the age we live in: the envious hatred of him who suffers want, and the selfish forgetfulness of him who lives in affluence.

All the enjoyment of my walk was gone; I left off looking about me, and retired into my own heart. The animated and moving sight in the streets gave place to inward meditation upon all the painful problems which have been written for the last four thousand years at the bottom of each human struggle, but which are propounded more clearly than ever in our days.

I pondered on the uselessness of so many contests, in which defeat and victory only displace each other by turns, and on the mistaken zealots who have repeated from generation to generation the bloody history of Cain and Abel; and, saddened with these mournful reflections, I walked on as chance took me, until the silence all around insensibly drew me out from my own thoughts.

I had reached one of the remote streets, in which those who would live in comfort and without ostentation, and who love serious reflection, delight to find a home. There were no shops along the dimly lighted street; one heard no sounds but of distant carriages, and of the steps of some of the inhabitants returning quietly home.

I instantly recognized the street, though I had been there only once before.

That was two years ago. I was walking at the time by the side of the Seine, to which the lights on the quays and bridges gave the aspect of a lake surrounded by a garland of stars; and I had reached the Louvre, when I was stopped by a crowd collected near the parapet they had gathered round a child of about six, who was crying, and I asked the cause of his tears.

"It seems that he was sent to walk in the Tuileries," said a mason, who was returning from his work with his trowel in his hand; "the servant who took care of him met with some friends there, and told the child to wait for him while he went to get a drink; but I suppose the drink made him more thirsty, for he has not come back, and the child cannot find his way home."

"Why do they not ask him his name, and where he lives?"

"They have been doing it for the last hour; but all he can say is, that he is called Charles, and that his father is Monsieur Duval – there are twelve hundred Duvals in Paris."

"Then he does not know in what part of the town he lives?"

"I should not think, indeed! Don't you see that he is a gentleman's child? He has never gone out except in a carriage or with a servant; he does not know what to do by himself."

Here the mason was interrupted by some of the voices rising above the others.

"We cannot leave him in the street," said some.

"The child-stealers would carry him off," continued others.

"We must take him to the overseer."

"Or to the police-office."

"That's the thing. Come, little one!"

But the child, frightened by these suggestions of danger, and at the names of police and overseer, cried louder, and drew back toward the parapet. In vain they tried to persuade him; his fears made him resist the more, and the most eager began to get weary, when the voice of a little boy was heard through the confusion.

"I know him well – I do," said he, looking at the lost child; "he belongs in our part of the town."

"What part is it?"

"Yonder, on the other side of the Boulevards – Rue des Magasins."

"And you have seen him before?"

"Yes, yes! he belongs to the great house at the end of the street, where there is an iron gate with gilt points."

The child quickly raised his head, and stopped crying. The little boy answered all the questions that were put to him, and gave such details as left no room for doubt. The other child understood him, for he went up to him as if to put himself under his protection.

"Then you can take him to his parents?" asked the mason, who had listened with real interest to the little boy's account.

"I don't care if I do," replied he; "it's the way I'm going."

"Then you will take charge of him?"

"He has only to come with me."

And, taking up the basket he had put down on the pavement, he set off toward the postern-gate of the Louvre.

The lost child followed him.

"I hope he will take him right," said I, when I saw them go away.

"Never fear," replied the mason; "the little one in the blouse is the same age as the other; but, as the saying is, he knows black from white;' poverty, you see, is a famous schoolmistress!"

The crowd dispersed. For my part, I went toward the Louvre; the thought came into my head to follow the two children, so as to guard against any mistake.

I was not long in overtaking them; they were walking side by side, talking, and already quite familiar with each other. The contrast in their dress then struck me. Little Duval wore one of those fanciful children's dresses which are expensive as well as in good taste; his coat was skillfully fitted to his figure, his trousers came down in plaits from his waist to his boots of polished leather with mother-of-pearl buttons, and his ringlets were half hid by a velvet cap. The appearance of his guide, on the contrary, was that of the class who dwell on the extreme borders of poverty, but who there maintain their ground with no surrender. His old blouse, patched with pieces of different shades, indicated the perseverance of an industrious mother struggling against the wear and tear of time; his trousers were become too short, and showed his stockings darned over and over again; and it was evident that his shoes were not made for him.

The countenances of the two children were not less different than their dress. That of the first was delicate and refined; his clear blue eye, his fair skin, and his smiling mouth gave him a charming look of innocence and happiness. The features of the other, on the contrary, had something rough in them; his eye was quick and lively, his complexion dark, his smile less merry than shrewd; all showed a mind sharpened by too early experience; he walked boldly through the middle of the streets thronged by carriages, and followed their countless turnings without hesitation.

I found, on asking him, that every day he carried dinner to his father, who was then working on the left bank of the Seine; and this responsible duty had made him careful and prudent. He had learned those hard but forcible lessons of necessity which nothing can equal or supply the place of. Unfortunately, the wants of his poor family had kept him from school, and he seemed to feel the loss; for he often stopped before the printshops, and asked his companion to read him the names of the engravings. In this way we reached the Boulevard Bonne Nouvelle, which the little wanderer seemed to know again. Notwithstanding his fatigue, he hurried on; he was agitated by mixed feelings; at the sight of his house he uttered a cry, and ran toward the iron gate with the gilt points; a lady who was standing at the entrance received him in her arms, and from the exclamations of joy, and the sound of kisses, I soon perceived she was his mother.

Not seeing either the servant or child return, she had sent in search of them in every direction, and was waiting for them in intense anxiety.

I explained to her in a few words what had happened. She thanked me warmly, and looked round for the little boy who had recognized and brought back her son; but while we were talking, he had disappeared.

It was for the first time since then that I had come into this part of Paris. Did the mother continue grateful? Had the children met again, and had the happy chance of their first meeting lowered between them that barrier which may mark the different ranks of men, but should not divide them?

While putting these questions to myself, I slackened my pace, and fixed my eyes on the great gate, which I just perceived. Suddenly I saw it open, and two children appeared at the entrance. Although much grown, I recognized them at first sight; they were the child who was found near the parapet of the Louvre, and his young guide. But the dress of the latter was greatly changed: his blouse of grey cloth was neat, and even spruce, and was fastened round the waist by a polished leather belt; he wore strong shoes, but made for his feet, and had on a new cloth cap. Just at the moment I saw him, he held in his two hands an enormous bunch of lilacs, to which his companion was trying to add narcissuses and primroses; the two children laughed, and parted with a friendly good-bye. M. Duval's son did not go in till he had seen the other turn the corner of the street.

Then I accosted the latter, and reminded him of our former meeting; he looked at me for a moment, and then seemed to recollect me.

"Forgive me if I do not make you a bow," said he, merrily, "but I want both my hands for the nosegay Monsieur Charles has given me."

"You are, then, become great friends?" said I.

"Oh! I should think so," said the child; "and now my father is rich too!"

"How's that?"

"Monsieur Duval lent him some money; he has taken a shop, where he works on his own account; and, as for me, I go to school."

"Yes," replied I, remarking for the first time the cross that decorated his little coat; "and I see that you are head-boy!"

"Monsieur Charles helps me to learn, and so I am come to be the first in the class."

"Are you now going to your lessons?"

"Yes, and he has given me some lilacs; for he has a garden where we play together, and where my mother can always have flowers."

"Then it is the same as if it were partly your own."

"So it is! Ah! they are good neighbors indeed. But here I am; good-bye, sir."

He nodded to me with a smile, and disappeared.

I went on with my walk, still pensive, but with a feeling of relief. If I had elsewhere witnessed the painful contrast between affluence and want, here I had found the true union of riches and poverty. Hearty good-will had smoothed down the more rugged inequalities on both sides, and had opened a road of true neighborhood and fellowship between the humble workshop and the stately mansion. Instead of hearkening to the voice of interest, they had both listened to that of self-sacrifice, and there was no place left for contempt or envy. Thus, instead of the beggar in rags, that I had seen at the other door cursing the rich man, I had found here the happy child of the laborer loaded with flowers and blessing him! The problem, so difficult and so dangerous to examine into with no regard but for the rights of it, I had just seen solved by love.

# *Chapter V*

## COMPENSATION

Sunday, May 27th

Capital cities have one thing peculiar to them: their days of rest seem to be the signal for a general dispersion and flight. Like birds that are just restored to liberty, the people come out of their stone cages, and joyfully fly toward the country. It is who shall find a green hillock for a seat, or the shade of a wood for a shelter; they gather May flowers, they run about the fields; the town is forgotten until the evening, when they return with sprigs of blooming hawthorn in their hats, and their hearts gladdened by pleasant thoughts and recollections of the past day; the next day they return again to their harness and to work.

These rural adventures are most remarkable at Paris. When the fine weather comes, clerks, shop keepers, and workingmen look forward impatiently for the Sunday as the day for trying a few hours of this pastoral life; they walk through six miles of grocers' shops and public-houses in the faubourgs, in the sole hope of finding a real turnip-field. The father of a family begins the practical education of his son by showing him wheat which has not taken the form of a loaf, and cabbage "in its wild state." Heaven only knows the encounters, the discoveries, the adventures that are met with! What Parisian has not had his Odyssey in an excursion through the suburbs, and would not be able to write a companion to the famous Travels by Land and by Sea from Paris to St. Cloud?

We do not now speak of that floating population from all parts, for whom our French Babylon is the caravansary of Europe: a phalanx of thinkers, artists, men of business, and travelers, who, like Homer's hero, have arrived in their intellectual country after beholding "many peoples and cities;" but of the settled Parisian, who keeps his appointed place, and lives on his own floor like the oyster on his rock, a curious vestige of the credulity, the slowness, and the simplicity of bygone ages.

For one of the singularities of Paris is, that it unites twenty populations completely different in character and manners. By the side of the gypsies of commerce and of art, who wander through all the several stages of fortune or fancy, live a quiet race of people with an independence, or with regular work, whose existence resembles the dial of a clock, on which the same hand points by turns to the same hours. If no other city can show more brilliant and more stirring forms of life, no other contains more obscure and more tranquil ones. Great cities are like the sea: storms agitate only the surface; if you go to the bottom, you find a region inaccessible to the tumult and the noise.

For my part, I have settled on the verge of this region, but do not actually live in it. I am removed from the turmoil of the world, and live in the shelter of solitude, but without being able to disconnect my thoughts from the struggle going on. I follow at a distance all its events of happiness or grief; I join the feasts and the funerals; for how can he who looks on, and knows what passes, do other than take part? Ignorance alone can keep us strangers to the life around us: selfishness itself will not suffice for that.

These reflections I made to myself in my attic, in the intervals of the various household works to which a bachelor is forced when he has no other servant than his own ready will. While I was pursuing my deductions, I had blacked my boots, brushed my coat, and tied my cravat; I had at last arrived at the important moment when we pronounce complacently that all is finished, and that well.

A grand resolve had just decided me to depart from my usual habits. The evening before, I had seen by the advertisements that the next day was a holiday at Sevres, and that the china manufactory would be open to the public. I was tempted by the beauty of the morning, and suddenly decided to go there.

On my arrival at the station on the left bank, I noticed the crowd hurrying on in the fear of being late. Railroads, besides many other advantages, possess that of teaching the French punctuality. They will submit to the clock when they are convinced that it is their master; they will learn to wait when they find they will not be waited for. Social virtues, are, in a great degree, good habits. How many great qualities are grafted into nations by their geographical position, by political necessity, and by institutions! Avarice was destroyed for a time among the Lacedaemonians by the creation of an iron coinage, too heavy and too bulky to be conveniently hoarded.

I found myself in a carriage with two middle-aged women belonging to the domestic and retired class of Parisians I have spoken of above. A few civilities were sufficient to gain me their confidence, and after some minutes I was acquainted with their whole history.

They were two poor sisters, left orphans at fifteen, and had lived ever since, as those who work for their livelihood must live, by economy and privation. For the last twenty or thirty years they had worked in jewelry in the same house; they had seen ten masters succeed one another, and make their fortunes in it, without any change in their own lot. They had always lived in the same room, at the end of one of the passages in the Rue St. Denis, where the air and the sun are unknown. They began their work before daylight, went on with it till after nightfall, and saw year succeed to year without their lives being marked by any other events than the Sunday service, a walk, or an illness.

The younger of these worthy work-women was forty, and obeyed her sister as she did when a child. The elder looked after her, took care of her, and scolded her with a mother's tenderness. At first it was amusing; afterward one could not help seeing something affecting in these two grey-haired children, one unable to leave off the habit of obeying, the other that of protecting.

And it was not in that alone that my two companions seemed younger than their years; they knew so little that their wonder never ceased. We had hardly arrived at Clamart before they involuntarily exclaimed, like the king in the children's game, that they "did not think the world was so great!"

It was the first time they had trusted themselves on a railroad, and it was amusing to see their sudden shocks, their alarms, and their courageous determinations: everything was a marvel to them! They had remains of youth within them, which made them sensible to things which usually only strike us in childhood. Poor creatures! they had still the feelings of another age, though they had lost its charms.

But was there not something holy in this simplicity, which had been preserved to them by abstinence from all the joys of life? Ah! accursed be he who first had the had courage to attach ridicule to that name of "old maid," which recalls so many images of grievous deception, of dreariness, and of abandonment! Accursed be he who can find a subject for sarcasm in involuntary misfortune, and who can crown grey hairs with thorns!

The two sisters were called Frances and Madeleine. This day's journey was a feat of courage without example in their lives. The fever of the times had infected them unawares. Yesterday Madeleine had suddenly proposed the idea of the expedition, and Frances had accepted it immediately. Perhaps it would have been better not to yield to the great temptation offered by her younger sister; but "we have our follies at all ages," as the prudent Frances philosophically remarked. As for Madeleine, there are no regrets or doubts for her; she is the life-guardsman of the establishment.

"We really must amuse ourselves," said she; "we live but once."

And the elder sister smiled at this Epicurean maxim. It was evident that the fever of independence was at its crisis in both of them.

And in truth it would have been a great pity if any scruple had interfered with their happiness, it was so frank and genial! The sight of the trees, which seemed to fly on both sides of the road, caused them unceasing admiration. The meeting a train passing in the contrary direction, with the noise and rapidity of a thunderbolt, made them shut their eyes and utter a cry; but it had already disappeared! They look around, take courage again, and express themselves full of astonishment at the marvel.

Madeleine declares that such a sight is worth the expense of the journey, and Frances would have agreed with her if she had not recollected, with some little alarm, the deficit which such an expense must make in their budget. The three francs spent upon this single expedition were the savings of a whole week of work. Thus the joy of the elder of the two sisters was mixed with remorse; the prodigal child now and then turned its eyes toward the back street of St. Denis.

But the motion and the succession of objects distract her. See the bridge of the Val surrounded by its lovely landscape: on the right, Paris with its grand monuments, which rise through the fog, or sparkle in the sun; on the left, Meudon, with its villas, its woods, its vines, and its royal castle! The two work-women look from one window to the other with exclamations of delight. One fellow-passenger laughs at their childish wonder; but to me it is deeply touching, for I see in it the sign of a long and monotonous seclusion: they are the prisoners of work, who have recovered liberty and fresh air for a few hours.

At last the train stops, and we get out. I show the two sisters the path that leads to Sevres, between the railway and the gardens, and they go on before, while I inquire about the time of returning.

I soon join them again at the next station, where they have stopped at the little garden belonging to the gatekeeper; both are already in deep conversation with him while he digs his garden-borders, and marks out the places for flower-seeds. He informs them that it is the time for hoeing out weeds, for making grafts and layers, for sowing annuals, and for destroying the insects on the rose trees. Madeleine has on the sill of her window two wooden boxes, in which, for want of air and sun, she has never been able to make anything grow but mustard and cress; but she persuades herself that, thanks to this information, all other plants may henceforth thrive in them. At last the gatekeeper, who is sowing a border with mignonette, gives her the rest of the seeds which he does not want, and the old maid goes off delighted, and begins to act over again the dream of Paired and her can of milk, with these flowers of her imagination.

On reaching the grove of acacias, where the fair was going on, I lost sight of the two sisters. I went alone among the sights: there were lotteries going on, mountebank shows, places for eating and drinking, and for shooting with the crossbow. I have always been struck by the spirit of these out-of-door festivities. In drawing room entertainments, people are cold, grave, often listless, and most of those who go there are brought together by habit or the obligations of society; in the country assemblies, on the contrary, you only find those who are attracted by the hope of enjoyment. There, it is a forced conscription; here, they are volunteers for gayety! Then, how easily they are pleased! How far this crowd of people is yet from knowing that to be pleased with nothing, and to look down on everything, is the height of fashion and good taste! Doubtless their amusements are often coarse; elegance and refinement are wanting in them; but at least they have heartiness. Oh, that the hearty enjoyments of these merry-makings could be retained in union with less vulgar feeling! Formerly religion stamped its holy character on the celebration of country festivals, and purified the pleasures without depriving them of their simplicity.

The hour arrives at which the doors of the porcelain manufactory and the museum of pottery are open to the public. I meet Frances and Madeleine again in the first room. Frightened at finding themselves in the midst of such regal magnificence, they hardly dare walk; they speak in a low tone, as if they were in a church.

"We are in the king's house," said the eldest sister, forgetting that there is no longer a king in France.

I encourage them to go on; I walk first, and they make up their minds to follow me.

What wonders are brought together in this collection! Here we see clay molded into every shape, tinted with every color, and combined with every sort of substance!

Earth and wood are the first substances worked upon by man, and seem more particularly meant for his use. They, like the domestic animals, are the essential accessories of his life; therefore there must be a more intimate connection between them and us. Stone and metals require long preparations; they resist our first efforts, and belong less to the individual than to communities. Earth and wood are, on the contrary, the principal instruments of the isolated being who must feed and shelter himself.

This, doubtless, makes me feel so much interested in the collection I am examining. These cups, so roughly modeled by the savage, admit me to a knowledge of some of his habits; these elegant yet incorrectly formed vases of the Indian tell me of a declining intelligence, – in which still glimmers the twilight of what was once bright sunshine; these jars, loaded with arabesques, show the fancy of the Arab rudely and ignorantly copied by the Spaniard! We find here the stamp of every race, every country, and every age.

My companions seemed little interested in these historical associations; they looked at all with that credulous admiration which leaves no room for examination or discussion. Madeleine read the name written under every piece of workmanship, and her sister answered with an exclamation of wonder.

In this way we reached a little courtyard, where they had thrown away the fragments of some broken china.

Frances perceived a colored saucer almost whole, of which she took possession as a record of the visit she was making; henceforth she would have a specimen of the Sevres china, "which is only made for kings!" I would not undeceive her by telling her that the products of the manufactory are sold all over the world, and that her saucer, before it was cracked, was the same as those that are bought at the shops for sixpence! Why should I destroy the illusions of her humble existence? Are we to break down the hedge-flowers that perfume our paths? Things are oftenest nothing in themselves; the thoughts we attach to them alone give them value. To rectify innocent mistakes, in order to recover some useless reality, is to be like those learned men who will see nothing in a plant but the chemical elements of which it is composed.

On leaving the manufactory, the two sisters, who had taken possession of me with the freedom of artlessness, invited me to share the luncheon they had brought with them. I declined at first, but they insisted with so much good nature, that I feared to pain them, and with some awkwardness gave way.

We had only to look for a convenient spot. I led them up the hill, and we found a plot of grass enameled with daisies, and shaded by two walnut trees.

Madeleine could not contain herself for joy. All her life she had dreamed of a dinner out on the grass! While helping her sister to take the provisions from the basket, she tells me of all her expeditions into the country that had been planned, and put off. Frances, on the other hand, was brought up at Montmorency, and before she became an orphan she had often gone back to her nurse's house. That which had the attraction of novelty for her sister, had for her the charm of recollection. She told of the vintage harvests to which her parents had taken her; the rides on Mother Luret's donkey, that they could not make go to the right without pulling him to the left; the cherry-gathering; and the sails on the lake in the innkeeper's boat.

These recollections have all the charm and freshness of childhood. Frances recalls to herself less what she has seen than what she has felt. While she is talking the cloth is laid, and we sit down under a tree. Before us winds the valley of Sevres, its many-storied houses abutting upon the gardens and the slopes of the hill; on the other side spreads out the park of St. Cloud, with its magnificent clumps of trees interspersed with meadows; above stretch the heavens like an immense ocean, in which the clouds are sailing! I look at this beautiful country, and I listen to these good old maids; I admire, and I am interested; and time passes gently on without my perceiving it.

At last the sun sets, and we have to think of returning. While Madeleine and Frances clear away the dinner, I walk down to the manufactory to ask the hour. The merrymaking is at its height; the blasts of the trombones resound from the band under the acacias. For a few moments I forget myself with looking about; but I have promised the two sisters to take them back to the Bellevue station; the train cannot wait, and I make haste to climb the path again which leads to the walnut trees.

Just before I reached them, I heard voices on the other side of the hedge. Madeleine and Frances were speaking to a poor girl whose clothes were burned, her hands blackened, and her face tied up with blood-stained bandages. I saw that she was one of the girls employed at the gunpowder mills, which are built further up on the common. An explosion had taken place a few days before; the girl's mother and elder sister were killed; she herself escaped by a miracle, and was now left without any means of support. She told all this with the resigned and unhopeful manner of one who has always been accustomed to suffer. The two sisters were much affected; I saw them consulting with each other in a low tone: then Frances took thirty sous out of a little coarse silk purse, which was all they had left, and gave them to the poor girl. I hastened on to that side of the hedge; but, before I reached it, I met the two old sisters, who called out to me that they would not return by the railway, but on foot!

I then understood that the money they had meant for the journey had just been given to the beggar! Good, like evil, is contagious: I run to the poor wounded girl, give her the sum that was to pay for my own place, and return to Frances and Madeleine, and tell them I will walk with them.

I am just come back from taking them home; and have left them delighted with their day, the recollection of which will long make them happy. This morning I was pitying those whose lives are obscure and joyless; now, I understand that God has provided a compensation with every trial. The smallest pleasure derives from rarity a relish otherwise unknown. Enjoyment is only what we feel to be such, and the luxurious man feels no longer: satiety has destroyed his appetite, while privation preserves to the other that first of earthly blessings: the being easily made happy. Oh, that I could persuade everyone of this! that so the rich might not abuse their riches, and that the poor might have patience. If happiness is the rarest of blessings, it is because the reception of it is the rarest of virtues.

Madeleine and Frances! ye poor old maids whose courage, resignation, and generous hearts are your only wealth, pray for the wretched who give themselves up to despair; for the unhappy who hate and envy; and for the unfeeling into whose enjoyments no pity enters.

# *Chapter VI*

## UNCLE MAURICE

June 7th, Four O'clock A.M.

I am not surprised at hearing, when I awake, the birds singing so joyfully outside my window; it is only by living, as they and I do, in a top story, that one comes to know how cheerful the mornings really are up among the roofs. It is there that the sun sends his first rays, and the breeze comes with the fragrance of the gardens and woods; there that a wandering butterfly sometimes ventures among the flowers of the attic, and that the songs of the industrious work-woman welcome the dawn of day. The lower stories are still deep in sleep, silence, and shadow, while here labor, light, and song already reign.

What life is around me! See the swallow returning from her search for food, with her beak full of insects for her young ones; the sparrows shake the dew from their wings while they chase one another in the sunshine; and my neighbors throw open their windows, and welcome the morning with their fresh faces! Delightful hour of waking, when everything returns to feeling and to motion; when the first light of day strikes upon creation, and brings it to life again, as the magic wand struck the palace of the Sleeping Beauty in the wood! It is a moment of rest from every misery; the sufferings of the sick are allayed, and a breath of hope enters into the hearts of the despairing. But, alas! it is but a short respite! Everything will soon resume its wonted course: the great human machine, with its long strains, its deep gasps, its collisions, and its crashes, will be again put in motion.

The tranquility of this first morning hour reminds me of that of our first years of life. Then, too, the sun shines brightly, the air is fragrant, and the illusions of youth-those birds of our life's morning-sing around us. Why do they fly away when we are older? Where do this sadness and this solitude, which gradually steal upon us, come from? The course seems to be the same with individuals and with communities: at starting, so readily made happy, so easily enchanted; and at the goal, the bitter disappointment or reality! The road, which began among hawthorns and primroses, ends speedily in deserts or in precipices! Why is there so much confidence at first, so much doubt at last? Has, then, the knowledge of life no other end but to make it unfit for happiness? Must we condemn ourselves to ignorance if we would preserve hope? Is the world and is the individual man intended, after all, to find rest only in an eternal childhood?

How many times have I asked myself these questions! Solitude has the advantage or the danger of making us continually search more deeply into the same ideas. As our discourse is only with ourself, we always give the same direction to the conversation; we are not called to turn it to the subject which occupies another mind, or interests another's feelings; and so an involuntary inclination makes us return forever to knock at the same doors!

I interrupted my reflections to put my attic in order. I hate the look of disorder, because it shows either a contempt for details or an unaptness for spiritual life. To arrange the things among which we have to live, is to establish the relation of property and of use between them and us: it is to lay the foundation of those habits without which man tends to the savage state. What, in fact, is social organization but a series of habits, settled in accordance with the dispositions of our nature?

I distrust both the intellect and the morality of those people to whom disorder is of no consequence – who can live at ease in an Augean stable. What surrounds us, reflects more or less that which is within us. The mind is like one of those dark lanterns which, in spite of everything, still throw some light around. If our tastes did not reveal our character, they would be no longer tastes, but instincts.

While I was arranging everything in my attic, my eyes rested on the little almanac hanging over my chimneypiece. I looked for the day of the month, and I saw these words written in large letters: "FÊTE DIEU!"

It is today! In this great city, where there are no longer any public religious solemnities, there is nothing to remind us of it; but it is, in truth, the period so happily chosen by the primitive church. "The day kept in honor of the Creator," says Châteaubriand, "happens at a time when the heaven and the earth declare His power, when the woods and fields are full of new life, and all are united by the happiest ties; there is not a single widowed plant in the fields."

What recollections these words have just awakened! I left off what I was about, I leaned my elbows on the windowsill, and, with my head between my two hands, I went back in thought to the little town where the first days of my childhood were passed.

The *Fête Dieu* was then one of the great events of my life! It was necessary to be diligent and obedient a long time beforehand, to deserve to share in it. I still recollect with what raptures of expectation I got up on the morning of the day. There was a holy joy in the air. The neighbors, up earlier than usual, hung cloths with flowers or figures, worked in tapestry, along the streets. I went from one to another, by turns admiring religious scenes of the Middle Ages, mythological compositions of the Renaissance, old battles in the style of Louis XIV, and the Arcadias of Madame de Pompadour. All this world of phantoms seemed to be coming forth from the dust of past ages, to assist – silent and motionless – at the holy ceremony. I looked, alternately in fear and wonder, at those terrible warriors with their swords always raised, those beautiful huntresses shooting the arrow which never left the bow, and those shepherds in satin breeches always playing the flute at the feet of the perpetually smiling shepherdess. Sometimes, when the wind blew behind these hanging pictures, it seemed to me that the figures themselves moved, and I watched to see them detach themselves from the wall, and take their places in the procession! But these impressions were vague and transitory. The feeling that predominated over every other was that of an overflowing yet quiet joy. In the midst of all the floating draperies, the scattered flowers, the voices of the maidens, and the gladness which, like a perfume, exhaled from everything, you felt transported in spite of yourself. The joyful sounds of the festival were repeated in your heart, in a thousand melodious echoes. You were more indulgent, more holy, more loving! For God was not only manifesting himself without, but also within us.

And then the altars for the occasion! the flowery arbors! the triumphal arches made of green boughs! What competition among the different parishes for the erection of the resting-places where the procession was to halt! It was who should contribute the rarest and the most beautiful of his possessions!

It was there I made my first sacrifice!

The wreaths of flowers were arranged, the candles lighted, and the Tabernacle dressed with roses; but one was wanting fit to crown the whole! All the neighboring gardens had been ransacked. I alone possessed a flower worthy of such a place. It was on the rose tree given me by my mother on my birthday. I had watched it for several months, and there was no other bud to blow on the tree. There it was, half open, in its mossy nest, the object of such long expectations, and of all a child's pride! I hesitated for some moments. No one had asked me for it; I might easily avoid losing it. I should hear no reproaches, but one rose noiselessly within me. When everyone else had given all they had, ought

I alone to keep back my treasure? Ought I to grudge to God one of the gifts which, like all the rest, I had received from him? At this last thought I plucked the flower from the stem, and took it to put at the top of the Tabernacle. Ah! why does the recollection of this sacrifice, which was so hard and yet so sweet to me, now make me smile? Is it so certain that the value of a gift is in itself, rather than in the intention? If the cup of cold water in the gospel is remembered to the poor man, why should not the flower be remembered to the child? Let us not look down upon the child's simple act of generosity; it is these which accustom the soul to self-denial and to sympathy. I cherished this moss-rose a long time as a sacred talisman; I had reason to cherish it always, as the record of the first victory won over myself.

It is now many years since I witnessed the celebration of the *Fête Dieu*; but should I again feel in it the happy sensations of former days? I still remember how, when the procession had passed, I walked through the streets strewed with flowers and shaded with green boughs. I felt intoxicated by the lingering perfumes of the incense, mixed with the fragrance of syringas, jasmine, and roses, and I seemed no longer to touch the ground as I went along. I smiled at everything; the whole world was Paradise in my eyes, and it seemed to me that God was floating in the air!

Moreover, this feeling was not the excitement of the moment: it might be more intense on certain days, but at the same time it continued through the ordinary course of my life. Many years thus passed for me in an expansion of heart, and a trustfulness which prevented sorrow, if not from coming, at least from staying with me. Sure of not being alone, I soon took heart again, like the child who recovers its courage, because it hears its mother's voice close by. Why have I lost that confidence of my childhood? Shall I never feel again so deeply that God is here?

How strange the association of our thoughts! A day of the month recalls my infancy, and see, all the recollections of my former years are growing up around me! Why was I so happy then? I consider well, and nothing is sensibly changed in my condition. I possess, as I did then, health and my daily bread; the only difference is, that I am now responsible for myself! As a child, I accepted life when it came; another cared and provided for me. So long as I fulfilled my present duties I was at peace within, and I left the future to the prudence of my father! My destiny was a ship, in the directing of which I had no share, and in which I sailed as a common passenger. There was the whole secret of childhood's happy security. Since then worldly wisdom has deprived me of it. When my lot was entrusted to my own and sole keeping, I thought to make myself master of it by means of a long insight into the future. I have filled the present hour with anxieties, by occupying my thoughts with the future; I have put my judgment in the place of Providence, and the happy child is changed into the anxious man.

A melancholy course, yet perhaps an important lesson. Who knows that, if I had trusted more to Him who rules the world, I should not have been spared all this anxiety? It may be that happiness is not possible here below, except on condition of living like a child, giving ourselves up to the duties of each day as it comes, and trusting in the goodness of our heavenly Father for all besides.

This reminds me of my Uncle Maurice! Whenever I have need to strengthen myself in all that is good, I turn my thoughts to him; I see again the gentle expression of his half-smiling, half-mournful face; I hear his voice, always soft and soothing as a breath of summer! The remembrance of him protects my life, and gives it light. He, too, was a saint and martyr here below. Others have pointed out the path of heaven; he has taught us to see those of earth aright.

But, except the angels, who are charged with noting down the sacrifices performed in secret, and the virtues which are never known, who has ever heard of my Uncle Maurice? Perhaps I alone remember his name, and still recall his history.

Well! I will write it, not for others, but for myself! They say that, at the sight of the Apollo, the body erects itself and assumes a more dignified attitude: in the same way, the soul should feel itself raised and ennobled by the recollection of a good man's life!

A ray of the rising sun lights up the little table on which I write; the breeze brings me in the scent of the mignonette, and the swallows wheel about my window with joyful twitterings. The image of my Uncle Maurice will be in its proper place amid the songs, the sunshine, and the fragrance.

Seven o'clock. – It is with men's lives as with days: some dawn radiant with a thousand colors, others dark with gloomy clouds. That of my Uncle Maurice was one of the latter. He was so sickly, when he came into the world, that they thought he must die; but notwithstanding these anticipations, which might be called hopes, he continued to live, suffering and deformed.

He was deprived of all joys as well as of all the attractions of childhood. He was oppressed because he was weak, and laughed at for his deformity. In vain the little hunchback opened his arms to the world: the world scoffed at him, and went its way.

However, he still had his mother, and it was to her that the child directed all the feelings of a heart repelled by others. With her he found shelter, and was happy, till he reached the age when a man must take his place in life; and Maurice had to content himself with that which others had refused with contempt. His education would have qualified him for any course of life; and he became an octroi-clerk* in one of the little toll-houses at the entrance of his native town.

He was always shut up in this dwelling of a few feet square, with no relaxation from the office accounts but reading and his mother's visits. On fine summer days she came to work at the door of his hut, under the shade of a clematis planted by Maurice. And, even when she was silent, her presence was a pleasant change for the hunchback; he heard the clinking of her long knitting-needles; he saw her mild and mournful profile, which reminded him of so many courageously-borne trials; he could every now and then rest his hand affectionately on that bowed neck, and exchange a smile with her!

This comfort was soon to be taken from him. His old mother fell sick, and at the end of a few days he had to give up all hope. Maurice was overcome at the idea of a separation which would henceforth leave him alone on earth, and abandoned himself to boundless grief. He knelt by the bedside of the dying woman, he called her by the fondest names, he pressed her in his arms, as if he could so keep her in life. His mother tried to return his caresses, and to answer him; but her hands were cold, her voice was already gone. She could only press her lips against the forehead of her son, heave a sigh, and close her eyes forever!

They tried to take Maurice away, but he resisted them and threw himself on that now motionless form.

"Dead!" cried he; "dead! She who had never left me, she who was the only one in the world who loved me! You, my mother, dead! What then remains for me here below?"

A stifled voice replied:

"God!"

Maurice, startled, raised himself! Was that a last sigh from the dead, or his own conscience, that had answered him? He did not seek to know, but he understood the answer, and accepted it.

It was then that I first knew him. I often went to see him in his little toll-house. He joined in my childish games, told me his finest stories, and let me gather his flowers. Deprived as he was of all external attractiveness, he showed himself full of kindness to all who came to him, and, though he never would put himself forward, he had a welcome for everyone. Deserted, despised, he submitted to everything with a gentle patience; and while he was thus stretched on the cross of life, amid the insults of his executioners, he repeated with Christ, "Father, forgive them, for they know not what they do."

* The octroi is the tax on provisions levied at the entrance of the town.

No other clerk showed so much honesty, zeal, and intelligence; but those who otherwise might have promoted him as his services deserved were repelled by his deformity. As he had no patrons, he found his claims were always disregarded. They preferred before him those who were better able to make themselves agreeable, and seemed to be granting him a favor when letting him keep the humble office which enabled him to live. Uncle Maurice bore injustice as he had borne contempt; unfairly treated by men, he raised his eyes higher, and trusted in the justice of Him who cannot be deceived.

He lived in an old house in the suburb, where many work-people, as poor but not as forlorn as he, also lodged. Among these neighbors there was a single woman, who lived by herself in a little garret, into which came both wind and rain. She was a young girl, pale, silent, and with nothing to recommend her but her wretchedness and her resignation to it. She was never seen speaking to any other woman, and no song cheered her garret. She worked without interest and without relaxation; a depressing gloom seemed to envelop her like a shroud. Her dejection affected Maurice; he attempted to speak to her; she replied mildly, but in few words. It was easy to see that she preferred her silence and her solitude to the little hunchback's good-will; he perceived it, and said no more.

But Toinette's needle was hardly sufficient for her support, and presently work failed her! Maurice learned that the poor girl was in want of everything, and that the tradesmen refused to give her credit. He immediately went to them privately and engaged to pay them for what they supplied Toinette with.

Things went on in this way for several months. The young dressmaker continued out of work, until she was at last frightened at the bills she had contracted with the shopkeepers. When she came to an explanation with them, everything was discovered. Her first impulse was to run to Uncle Maurice, and thank him on her knees. Her habitual reserve had given way to a burst of deepest feeling. It seemed as if gratitude had melted all the ice of that numbed heart.

Being now no longer embarrassed with a secret, the little hunchback could give greater efficacy to his good offices. Toinette became to him a sister, for whose wants he had a right to provide. It was the first time since the death of his mother that he had been able to share his life with another. The young woman received his attentions with feeling, but with reserve. All Maurice's efforts were insufficient to dispel her gloom: she seemed touched by his kindness, and sometimes expressed her sense of it with warmth; but there she stopped. Her heart was a closed book, which the little hunchback might bend over, but could not read. In truth he cared little to do so; he gave himself up to the happiness of being no longer alone, and took Toinette such as her long trials had made her; he loved her as she was, and wished for nothing else but still to enjoy her company.

This thought insensibly took possession of his mind, to the exclusion of all besides. The poor girl was as forlorn as himself; she had become accustomed to the deformity of the hunchback, and she seemed to look on him with an affectionate sympathy! What more could he wish for? Until then, the hopes of making himself acceptable to a helpmate had been repelled by Maurice as a dream; but chance seemed willing to make it a reality. After much hesitation he took courage, and decided to speak to her.

It was evening; the little hunchback, in much agitation, directed his steps toward the work-woman's garret just as he was about to enter, he thought he heard a strange voice pronouncing the maiden's name. He quickly pushed open the door, and perceived Toinette weeping, and leaning on the shoulder of a young man in the dress of a sailor.

At the sight of my uncle, she disengaged herself quickly, and ran to him, crying out:

"Ah! come in – come in! It is he that I thought was dead: it is Julien; it is my betrothed!"

Maurice tottered, and drew back. A single word had told him all!

It seemed to him as if the ground shook and his heart was about to break; but the same voice that he had heard by his mother's deathbed again sounded in his ears, and he soon recovered himself. God was still his friend!

He himself accompanied the newly-married pair on the road when they left the town, and, after wishing them all the happiness which was denied to him, he returned with resignation to the old house in the suburb.

It was there that he ended his life, forsaken by men, but not as he said by the Father which is in heaven. He felt His presence everywhere; it was to him in the place of all else. When he died, it was with a smile, and like an exile setting out for his own country. He who had consoled him in poverty and ill-health, when he was suffering from injustice and forsaken by all, had made death a gain and blessing to him.

Eight o'clock. – All I have just written has pained me! Till now I have looked into life for instruction how to live. Is it then true that human maxims are not always sufficient? that beyond goodness, prudence, moderation, humility, self-sacrifice itself, there is one great truth, which alone can face great misfortunes? and that, if man has need of virtues for others, he has need of religion for himself?

When, in youth, we drink our wine with a merry heart, as the Scripture expresses it, we think we are sufficient for ourselves; strong, happy, and beloved, we believe, like Ajax, we shall be able to escape every storm in spite of the gods. But later in life, when the back is bowed, when happiness proves a fading flower, and the affections grow chill-then, in fear of the void and the darkness, we stretch out our arms, like the child overtaken by night, and we call for help to Him who is everywhere.

I was asking this morning why this growing confusion alike for society and for the individual? In vain does human reason from hour to hour light some new torch on the roadside: the night continues to grow ever darker! Is it not because we are content to withdraw farther and farther from God, the Sun of spirits?

But what do these hermit's reveries signify to the world? The inward turmoils of most men are stifled by the outward ones; life does not give them time to question themselves. Have they time to know what they are, and what they should be, whose whole thoughts are in the next lease or the last price of stock? Heaven is very high, and wise men look only at the earth.

But I – poor savage amid all this civilization, who seek neither power nor riches, and who have found in my own thoughts the home and shelter of my spirit – I can go back with impunity to these recollections of my childhood; and, if this our great city no longer honors the name of God with a festival, I will strive still to keep the feast to Him in my heart.

# *Chapter VII*

## THE PRICE OF POWER AND THE WORTH OF FAME

Sunday, July 1st

Yesterday the month dedicated to Juno (Junius, June) by the Romans ended. Today we enter on July.

In ancient Rome this latter month was called Quintiles (the fifth), because the year, which was then divided into only ten parts, began in March. When Numa Pompilius divided it into twelve months this name of Quintiles was preserved, as well as those that followed – Sexteles, September, October, November, December – although these designations did not accord with the newly arranged order of the months. At last, after a time the month Quintiles, in which Julius Caesar was born, was called Julius, whence we have July. Thus this name, placed in the calendar, is become the imperishable record of a great man; it is an immortal epitaph on Time's highway, engraved by the admiration of man.

How many similar inscriptions are there! Seas, continents, mountains, stars, and monuments, have all in succession served the same purpose! We have turned the whole world into a Golden Book, like that in which the state of Venice used to enroll its illustrious names and its great deeds. It seems that mankind feels a necessity for honoring itself in its elect ones, and that it raises itself in its own eyes by choosing heroes from among its own race. The human family love to preserve the memory; of the parvenus of glory, as we cherish that of a great ancestor, or of a benefactor.

In fact, the talents granted to a single individual do not benefit himself alone, but are gifts to the world; everyone shares them, for everyone suffers or benefits by his actions. Genius is a lighthouse, meant to give light from afar; the man who bears it is but the rock upon which this lighthouse is built.

I love to dwell upon these thoughts; they explain to me in what consists our admiration for glory. When glory has benefited men, that admiration is gratitude; when it is only remarkable in itself, it is the pride of race; as men, we love to immortalize the most shining examples of humanity.

Who knows whether we do not obey the same instinct in submitting to the hand of power? Apart from the requirements of a gradation of ranks, or the consequences of a conquest, the multitude delight to surround their chiefs with privileges – whether it be that their vanity makes them thus to aggrandize one of their own creations, or whether they try to conceal the humiliation of subjection by exaggerating the importance of those who rule them. They wish to honor themselves through their master; they elevate him on their shoulders as on a pedestal; they surround him with a halo of light, in order that some of it may be reflected upon themselves. It is still the fable of the dog who contents himself with the chain and collar, so that they are of gold.

This servile vanity is not less natural or less common than the vanity of dominion. Whoever feels himself incapable of command, at least desires to obey a powerful chief. Serfs have been known to consider themselves dishonored when they became the property of a mere count after having been that of a prince, and Saint-Simon mentions a valet who would only wait upon marquises.

July 7th, seven o'clock P. M. – I have just now been up the Boulevards; it was the opera night, and there was a crowd of carriages in the Rue Lepelletier. The foot-passengers who were stopped at a crossing recognized the persons in some of these as we went by, and mentioned their names; they were those of celebrated or powerful men, the successful ones of the day.

Near me there was a man looking on with hollow cheeks and eager eyes, whose thin black coat was threadbare. He followed with envious looks these possessors of the privileges of power or of fame, and I read on his lips, which curled with a bitter smile, all that passed in his mind.

"Look at them, the lucky fellows!" thought he; "all the pleasures of wealth, all the enjoyments of pride, are theirs. Their names are renowned, all their wishes fulfilled; they are the sovereigns of the world, either by their intellect or their power; and while I, poor and unknown, toil painfully along the road below, they wing their way over the mountain-tops gilded by the broad sunshine of prosperity."

I have come home in deep thought. Is it true that there are these inequalities, I do not say in the fortunes, but in the happiness of men? Do genius and authority really wear life as a crown, while the greater part of mankind receive it as a yoke? Is the difference of rank but a different use of men's dispositions and talents, or a real inequality in their destinies? A solemn question, as it regards the verification of God's impartiality.

July 8th, noon. – I went this morning to call upon a friend from the same province as myself, who is the first usher-in-waiting to one of our ministers. I took him some letters from his family, left for him by a traveler just come from Brittany. He wished me to stay.

"Today," said he, "the Minister gives no audience: he takes a day of rest with his family. His younger sisters are arrived; he will take them this morning to St. Cloud, and in the evening he has invited his friends to a private ball. I shall be dismissed directly for the rest of the day. We can dine together; read the news while you are waiting for me."

I sat down at a table covered with newspapers, all of which I looked over by turns. Most of them contained severe criticisms on the last political acts of the minister; some of them added suspicions as to the honor of the minister himself.

Just as I had finished reading, a secretary came for them to take them to his master.

He was then about to read these accusations, to suffer silently the abuse of all those tongues which were holding him up to indignation or to scorn! Like the Roman victor in his triumph, he had to endure the insults of him who followed his car, relating to the crowd his follies, his ignorance, or his vices.

But, among the arrows shot at him from every side, would no one be found poisoned? Would not one reach some spot in his heart where the wound would be incurable? What is the worth of a life exposed to the attacks of envious hatred or furious conviction? The Christians yielded only the fragments of their flesh to the beasts of the amphitheaters; the man in power gives up his peace, his affections, his honor, to the cruel bites of the pen.

While I was musing upon these dangers of greatness, the usher entered hastily. Important news had been received: the minister is just summoned to the council; he will not be able to take his sisters to St. Cloud.

I saw, through the windows, the young ladies, who were waiting at the door, sorrowfully go upstairs again, while their brother went off to the council. The carriage, which should have gone filled with so much family happiness, is just out of sight, carrying only the cares of a statesman in it.

The usher came back discontented and disappointed. The more or less of liberty which he is allowed to enjoy, is his barometer of the political atmosphere. If he gets leave, all goes well; if he is kept at his post, the country is in danger. His opinion on public affairs is but a calculation of his own interest. My friend is almost a statesman.

I had some conversation with him, and he told me several curious particulars of public life.

The new minister has old friends whose opinions he opposes, though he still retains his personal regard for them. Though separated from them by the colors he fights under, they remain united by old associations; but the exigencies of party forbid him to meet them. If their intercourse continued, it would awaken suspicion; people would imagine that some dishonorable bargain was going on; his friends would be held to be traitors desirous to sell themselves, and he the corrupt minister prepared to buy them. He has, therefore, been obliged to break off friendships of twenty years' standing, and to sacrifice attachments which had become a second nature.

Sometimes, however, the minister still gives way to his old feelings; he receives or visits his friends privately; he shuts himself up with them, and talks of the times when they could be open friends. By dint of precautions they have hitherto succeeded in concealing this blot of friendship against policy; but sooner or later the newspapers will be informed of it, and will denounce him to the country as an object of distrust.

For whether hatred be honest or dishonest, it never shrinks from any accusation. Sometimes it even proceeds to crime. The usher assured me that several warnings had been given the minister which had made him fear the vengeance of an assassin, and that he no longer ventured out on foot.

Then, from one thing to another, I learned what temptations came in to mislead or overcome his judgment; how he found himself fatally led into obliquities which he could not but deplore. Misled by passion, overpersuaded by entreaties, or compelled for reputation's sake, he has many times held the balance with an unsteady hand. How sad the condition of him who is in authority! Not only are the miseries of power imposed upon him, but its vices also, which, not content with torturing, succeed in corrupting him.

We prolonged our conversation till it was interrupted by the minister's return. He threw himself out of the carriage with a handful of papers, and with an anxious manner went into his own room. An instant afterward his bell was heard; his secretary was called to send off notices to all those invited for the evening; the ball would not take place; they spoke mysteriously of bad news transmitted by the telegraph, and in such circumstances an entertainment would seem to insult the public sorrow.

I took leave of my friend, and here I am at home. What I have just seen is an answer to my doubts the other day. Now I know with what pangs men pay for their dignities; now I understand

That Fortune sells what we believe she gives.

This explains to me the reason why Charles V. aspired to the repose of the cloister.

And yet I have only glanced at some of the sufferings attached to power. What shall I say of the falls in which its possessors are precipitated from the heights of heaven to the very depths of the earth? of that path of pain along which they must forever bear the burden of their responsibility? of that chain of decorums and ennuis which encompasses every act of their lives, and leaves them so little liberty?

The partisans of despotism adhere with reason to forms and ceremonies. If men wish to give unlimited power to their fellow-man, they must keep him separated from ordinary humanity; they must surround him with a continual worship, and, by a constant ceremonial, keep up for him the superhuman part they have granted him. Our masters cannot remain absolute, except on condition of being treated as idols.

But, after all, these idols are men, and, if the exclusive life they must lead is an insult to the dignity of others, it is also a torment to themselves. Everyone knows the law of the Spanish court, which used to regulate, hour by hour, the actions of the king and queen; "so that," says Voltaire, "by reading it one can tell all that the sovereigns of Spain have done, or will do, from Philip II to the day of judgment." It was by this law that Philip III, when sick, was obliged to endure such an excess of heat that he died in consequence, because the Duke of Uzeda, who alone had the right to put out the fire in the royal chamber, happened to be absent.

When the wife of Charles II was run away with on a spirited horse, she was about to perish before anyone dared to save her, because etiquette forbade them to touch the queen. Two young officers endangered their lives for her by stopping the horse. The prayers and tears of her whom they had just snatched from death were necessary to obtain pardon for their crime. Everyone knows the anecdote related by Madame Campan of Marie Antoinette, wife of Louis XVI. One day, being at her toilet, when the chemise was about to be presented to her by one of the assistants, a lady of very ancient family entered and claimed the honor, as she had the right by etiquette; but, at the moment she was about to fulfill her duty, a lady of higher rank appeared, and in her turn took the garment she was about to offer to the queen; when a third lady of still higher title came in her turn, and was followed by a fourth, who was no other than the king's sister. The chemise was in this manner passed from hand to hand, with ceremonies, courtesies, and compliments, before it came to the queen, who, half naked and quite ashamed, was shivering with cold for the great honor of etiquette.

12th, seven o'clock, P.M. – On coming home this evening, I saw, standing at the door of a house, an old man, whose appearance and features reminded me of my father. There was the same beautiful smile, the same deep and penetrating eye, the same noble bearing of the head, and the same careless attitude.

I began living over again the first years of my life, and recalling to myself the conversations of that guide whom God in his mercy had given me, and whom in his severity he had too soon withdrawn.

When my father spoke, it was not only to bring our two minds together by an interchange of thought, but his words always contained instruction.

Not that he endeavored to make me feel it so: my father feared everything that had the appearance of a lesson. He used to say that virtue could make herself devoted friends, but she did not take pupils: therefore he was not desirous to teach goodness; he contented himself with sowing the seeds of it, certain that experience would make them grow.

How often has good grain fallen thus into a corner of the heart, and, when it has been long forgotten, all at once put forth the blade and come into ear! It is a treasure laid aside in a time of ignorance, and we do not know its value till we find ourselves in need of it.

Among the stories with which he enlivened our walks or our evenings, there is one which now returns to my memory, doubtless because the time is come to derive its lesson from it.

My father, who was apprenticed at the age of twelve to one of those trading collectors who call themselves naturalists, because they put all creation under glasses that they may sell it by retail, had always led a life of poverty and labor. Obliged to rise before daybreak, by turns shop-boy, clerk, and laborer, he was made to bear alone all the work of a trade of which his master reaped all the profits. In truth, this latter had a peculiar talent for making the most of the labor of other people. Though unfit himself for the execution of any kind of work, no one knew better how to sell it. His words were a net, in which people found themselves taken before they were aware. And since he was devoted to himself alone, and looked on the producer as his enemy, and the buyer as prey, he used them both with that obstinate perseverance which avarice teaches.

My father was a slave all the week, and could call himself his own only on Sunday. The master naturalist, who used to spend the day at the house of an old female relative, then gave him his liberty on condition that he dined out, and at his own expense. But my father used secretly to take with him a crust of bread, which he hid in his botanizing-box, and, leaving Paris as soon as it was day, he would wander far into the valley of Montmorency, the wood of Meudon, or among the windings of the Marne. Excited by the fresh air, the penetrating perfume of the growing vegetation, or the fragrance of the honeysuckles, he would walk on until hunger or fatigue made itself felt. Then he would sit under a hedge, or by the side of a stream, and would make a rustic feast, by turns on watercresses, wood strawberries, and blackberries picked from the hedges; he would gather a few plants, read a few pages of Florian, then in greatest vogue, of Gessner, who was just translated, or of Jean Jacques, of whom he possessed three old volumes. The day was thus passed alternately in activity and rest, in pursuit and meditation, until the declining sun warned him to take again the road to Paris, where he would arrive, his feet torn and dusty, but his mind invigorated for a whole week.

One day, as he was going toward the wood of Viroflay, he met, close to it, a stranger who was occupied in botanizing and in sorting the plants he had just gathered. He was an elderly man with an honest face; but his eyes, which were rather deep-set under his eyebrows, had a somewhat uneasy and timid expression. He was dressed in a brown cloth coat, a grey waistcoat, black breeches, and worsted stockings, and held an ivory-headed cane under his arm. His appearance was that of a small retired tradesman who was living on his means, and rather below the golden mean of Horace.

My father, who had great respect for age, civilly raised his hat to him as he passed. In doing so, a plant he held fell from his hand; the stranger stooped to take it up, and recognized it.

"It is a Deutaria heptaphyllos," said he; "I have not yet seen any of them in these woods; did you find it near here, sir?"

My father replied that it was to be found in abundance on the top of the hill, toward Sevres, as well as the great Laserpitium.

"That, too!" repeated the old man more briskly. "Ah! I shall go and look for them; I have gathered them formerly on the hillside of Robaila."

My father proposed to take him. The stranger accepted his proposal with thanks, and hastened to collect together the plants he had gathered; but all of a sudden he appeared seized with a scruple. He observed to his companion that the road he was going was halfway up the hill, and led in the direction of the castle of the Dames Royales at Bellevue; that by going to the top he would consequently turn out of his road, and that it was not right he should take this trouble for a stranger.

My father insisted upon it with his habitual good nature; but, the more eagerness he showed, the more obstinately the old man refused; it even seemed to my father that his good intention at last excited his suspicion. He therefore contented himself with pointing out the road to the stranger, whom he saluted, and he soon lost sight of him.

Many hours passed by, and he thought no more of the meeting. He had reached the copses of Chaville, where, stretched on the ground in a mossy glade, he read once more the last volume of Émile. The delight of reading it had so completely absorbed him that he had ceased to see or hear anything around him. With his cheeks flushed and his eyes moist, he repeated aloud a passage which had particularly affected him.

An exclamation uttered close by him awoke him from his ecstasy; he raised his head, and perceived the tradesman-looking person he had met before on the crossroad at Viroflay.

He was loaded with plants, the collection of which seemed to have put him into high good-humor.

"A thousand thanks, sir," said he to my father. "I have found all that you told me of, and I am indebted to you for a charming walk."

My father respectfully rose, and made a civil reply. The stranger had grown quite familiar, and even asked if his young "brother botanist" did not think of returning to Paris. My father replied in the affirmative, and opened his tin box to put his book back in it.

The stranger asked him with a smile if he might without impertinence ask the name of it. My father answered that it was Rousseau's Émile.

The stranger immediately became grave.

They walked for some time side by side, my father expressing, with the warmth of a heart still throbbing with emotion, all that this work had made him feel; his companion remaining cold and silent. The former extolled the glory of the great Genevese writer, whose genius had made him a citizen of the world; he expatiated on this privilege of great thinkers, who reign in spite of time and space, and gather together a people of willing subjects out of all nations; but the stranger suddenly interrupted him:

"And how do you know," said he, mildly, "whether Jean Jacques would not exchange the reputation which you seem to envy for the life of one of the wood-cutters whose chimneys' smoke we see? What has fame brought him except persecution? The unknown friends whom his books may have made for him content themselves with blessing him in their hearts, while the declared enemies that they have drawn upon him pursue him with violence and calumny! His pride has been flattered by success: how many times has it been wounded by satire? And be assured that human pride is like the Sybarite who was prevented from sleeping by a crease in a roseleaf. The activity of a vigorous mind, by which the world profits, almost always turns against him who possesses it. He expects more from it as he grows older; the ideal he pursues continually disgusts him with the actual; he is like a man who, with a too-refined sight, discerns spots and blemishes in the most beautiful face. I will not speak of stronger temptations and of deeper downfalls. Genius, you have said, is a kingdom; but what virtuous man is not afraid of being a king? He who feels only his great powers, is – with the weaknesses and passions of our nature – preparing for great failures. Believe me, sir, the unhappy man who wrote this book is no object of admiration or of envy; but, if you have a feeling heart, pity him!"

My father, astonished at the excitement with which his companion pronounced these last words, did not know what to answer.

Just then they reached the paved road which led from Meudon Castle to that of Versailles; a carriage was passing.

The ladies who were in it perceived the old man, uttered an exclamation of surprise, and leaning out of the window repeated:

"There is Jean Jacques – there is Rousseau!"

Then the carriage disappeared in the distance.

My father remained motionless, confounded, and amazed, his eyes wide open, and his hands clasped.

Rousseau, who had shuddered on hearing his name spoken, turned toward him:

"You see," said he, with the bitter misanthropy which his later misfortunes had produced in him, "Jean Jacques cannot even hide himself: he is an object of curiosity to some, of malignity to others, and to all he is a public thing, at which they point the finger. It would signify less if he had only to submit to the impertinence of the idle; but, as soon as a man has had the misfortune to make himself a name, he becomes public property. Everyone rakes into his life, relates his most trivial actions, and insults his feelings; he becomes like those walls, which every passer-by may deface with some abusive writing. Perhaps you will say that I have myself encouraged this curiosity by publishing my Confessions. But the world forced me to it. They looked into my house through the blinds, and they slandered me; I have opened the doors and windows, so that they should at least know me such as I am. Adieu, sir. Whenever you wish to know the worth of fame, remember that you have seen Rousseau."

Nine o'clock. – Ah! now I understand my father's story! It contains the answer to one of the questions I asked myself a week ago. Yes, I now feel that fame and power are gifts that are dearly bought; and that, when they dazzle the soul, both are oftenest, as Madame de Stael says, but *un deuil eclatant de bonheur!*

'Tis better to be lowly born,
And range with humble livers in content,
Than to be perk'd up in a glistering grief,
And wear a golden sorrow.*

---

* Henry VIII., Act II., Scene 3.

# *Chapter VIII*

## MISANTHROPY AND REPENTANCE

August 3d, Nine O'clock P.M.

There are days when everything appears gloomy to us; the world, like the sky, is covered by a dark fog. Nothing seems in its place; we see only misery, improvidence, and cruelty; the world seems without God, and given up to all the evils of chance.

Yesterday I was in this unhappy humor. After a long walk in the faubourgs, I returned home, sad and dispirited.

Everything I had seen seemed to accuse the civilization of which we are so proud! I had wandered into a little by-street, with which I was not acquainted, and I found myself suddenly in the middle of those dreadful abodes where the poor are born, to languish and die. I looked at those decaying walls, which time has covered with a foul leprosy; those windows, from which dirty rags hang out to dry; those fetid gutters, which coil along the fronts of the houses like venomous reptiles! I felt oppressed with grief, and hastened on.

A little farther on I was stopped by the hearse of a hospital; a dead man, nailed down in his deal coffin, was going to his last abode, without funeral pomp or ceremony, and without followers. There was not here even that last friend of the outcast – the dog, which a painter has introduced as the sole attendant at the pauper's burial! He whom they were preparing to commit to the earth was going to the tomb, as he had lived, alone; doubtless no one would be aware of his end. In this battle of society, what signifies a soldier the less?

But what, then, is this human society, if one of its members can thus disappear like a leaf carried away by the wind?

The hospital was near a barrack, at the entrance of which old men, women, and children were quarreling for the remains of the coarse bread which the soldiers had given them in charity! Thus, beings like ourselves daily wait in destitution on our compassion till we give them leave to live! Whole troops of outcasts, in addition to the trials imposed on all

God's children, have to endure the pangs of cold, hunger, and humiliation. Unhappy human commonwealth! Where man is in a worse condition than the bee in its hive, or the ant in its subterranean city!

Ah! what then avails our reason? What is the use of so many high faculties, if we are neither the wiser nor the happier for them? Which of us would not exchange his life of labor and trouble with that of the birds of the air, to whom the whole world is a life of joy?

How well I understand the complaint of Mao, in the popular tales of the *Foyer Breton* who, when dying of hunger and thirst, says, as he looks at the bullfinches rifling the fruit trees:

"Alas! those birds are happier than Christians; they have no need of inns, or butchers, or bakers, or gardeners. God's heaven belongs to them, and earth spreads a continual feast before them! The tiny flies are their game, ripe grass their cornfields, and hips and haws their store of fruit. They have the right of taking everywhere, without paying or asking leave: thus comes it that the little birds are happy, and sing all the livelong day!"

But the life of man in a natural state is like that of the birds; he equally enjoys nature. "The earth spreads a continual feast before him." What, then, has he gained by that selfish and imperfect association which forms a nation? Would it not be better for everyone to turn again to the fertile bosom of nature, and live there upon her bounty in peace and liberty?

August 20th, four o'clock A.M. – The dawn casts a red glow on my bed-curtains; the breeze brings in the fragrance of the gardens below. Here I am again leaning on my elbows by the windows, inhaling the freshness and gladness of this first wakening of the day.

My eye always passes over the roofs filled with flowers, warbling, and sunlight, with the same pleasure; but today it stops at the end of a buttress which separates our house from the next.

The storms have stripped the top of its plaster covering, and dust carried by the wind has collected in the crevices, and, being fixed there by the rain, has formed a sort of aërial terrace, where some green grass has sprung up. Among it rises a stalk of wheat, which today is surmounted by a sickly ear that droops its yellow head.

This poor stray crop on the roofs, the harvest of which will fall to the neighboring sparrows, has carried my thoughts to the rich crops which are now falling beneath the sickle; it has recalled to me the beautiful walks I took as a child through my native province, when the threshing-floors at the farmhouses resounded from every part with the sound of a flail, and when the carts, loaded with golden sheaves, came in by all the roads. I still remember the songs of the maidens, the cheerfulness of the old men, the open-hearted merriment of the laborers. There was, at that time, something in their looks both of pride and feeling. The latter came from thankfulness to God, the former from the sight of the harvest, the reward of their labor. They felt indistinctly the grandeur and the holiness of their part in the general work of the world; they looked with pride upon their mountains of corn-sheaves, and they seemed to say, Next to God, it is we who feed the world!

What a wonderful order there is in all human labor!

While the husbandman furrows his land, and prepares for everyone his daily bread, the town artisan, far away, weaves the stuff in which he is to be clothed; the miner seeks underground the iron for his plow; the soldier defends him against the invader; the judge takes care that the law protects his fields; the tax-comptroller adjusts his private interests with those of the public; the merchant occupies himself in exchanging his products with those of distant countries; the men of science and of art add every day a few horses to this ideal team, which draws along the material world, as steam impels the gigantic trains of our iron roads! Thus all unite together, all help one another; the toil of each one benefits himself and all the world; the work has been apportioned among the different members of the whole of society by a tacit agreement. If, in this apportionment, errors are committed, if certain individuals have not been employed according to their capacities, those defects of detail diminish in the sublime conception of the whole. The poorest man included in this association has his place, his work, his reason for being there; each is something in the whole.

There is nothing like this for man in the state of nature. As he depends only upon himself, it is necessary that he be sufficient for everything. All creation is his property; but he finds in it as many hindrances as helps. He must surmount these obstacles with the single strength that God has given him; he cannot reckon on any other aid than chance and opportunity. No one reaps, manufactures, fights, or thinks for him; he is nothing to anyone. He is a unit multiplied by the cipher of his own single powers; while the civilized man is a unit multiplied by the whole of society.

But, notwithstanding this, the other day, disgusted by the sight of some vices in detail, I cursed the latter, and almost envied the life of the savage.

One of the infirmities of our nature is always to mistake feeling for evidence, and to judge of the season by a cloud or a ray of sunshine.

Was the misery, the sight of which made me regret a savage life, really the effect of civilization? Must we accuse society of having created these evils, or acknowledge, on the contrary, that it has alleviated them? Could the women and children, who were receiving the coarse bread from the soldier, hope in the desert for more help or pity? That dead man, whose forsaken state I deplored, had he not found, by the cares of a hospital, a coffin and the humble grave where he was about to rest? Alone, and far from men, he would have died like the wild beast in his den, and would now be serving as food for vultures! These benefits of human society are shared, then, by the most destitute. Whoever eats the bread that another has reaped and kneaded, is under an obligation to his brother, and cannot say he owes him nothing in return. The poorest of us has received from society much more than his own single strength would have permitted him to wrest from nature.

But cannot society give us more? Who doubts it? Errors have been committed in this distribution of tasks and workers. Time will diminish the number of them; with new lights a better division will arise; the elements of society go on toward perfection, like everything else. The difficulty is to know how to adapt ourselves to the slow step of time, whose progress can never be forced on without danger.

August 14th, six o'clock A.M. – My garret window rises upon the roof like a massive watchtower. The corners are covered by large sheets of lead, which run into the tiles; the successive action of cold and heat has made them rise, and so a crevice has been formed in an angle on the right side. There a sparrow has built her nest.

I have followed the progress of this aërial habitation from the first day. I have seen the bird successively bring the straw, moss, and wool designed for the construction of her abode; and I have admired the persevering skill she expended in this difficult work. At first, my new neighbor spent her days in fluttering over the poplar in the garden, and in chirping along the gutters; a fine lady's life seemed the only one to suit her. Then all of a sudden, the necessity of preparing a shelter for her brood transformed our idler into a worker; she no longer gave herself either rest or relaxation. I saw her always either flying, fetching, or carrying; neither rain nor sun stopped her. A striking example of the power of necessity! We are indebted to it not only for most of our talents, but for many of our virtues!

Is it not necessity that has given the people of less favored climates that constant activity which has placed them so quickly at the head of nations? As they are deprived of most of the gifts of nature, they have supplied them by their industry; necessity has sharpened their understanding, endurance awakened their foresight. While elsewhere man, warmed by an ever brilliant sun, and loaded with the bounties of the earth, was remaining poor, ignorant, and naked, in the midst of gifts he did not attempt to explore, here he was forced by necessity to wrest his food from the ground, to build habitations to defend himself from the intemperance of the weather, and to warm his body by clothing himself with the wool of animals. Work makes him both more intelligent and more robust: disciplined by it, he seems to mount higher on the ladder of creation, while those more favored by nature remain on the step nearest to the brutes.

I made these reflections while looking at the bird, whose instinct seemed to have become more acute since she had been occupied in work. At last the nest was finished; she set up her household there, and I followed her through all the phases of her new existence.

When she had sat on the eggs, and the young ones were hatched, she fed them with the most attentive care. The corner of my window had become a stage of moral action, which fathers and mothers might come to take lessons from. The little ones soon became large, and this morning I have seen them take their first flight. One of them, weaker than the others, was not able to clear the edge of the roof, and fell into the gutter. I caught him with some difficulty, and placed him again on the tile in front of his house, but the mother has not noticed him. Once freed from the cares of a family, she has resumed her wandering life among the trees and along the roofs. In vain I have kept away from my window, to take from her every excuse for fear; in vain the feeble little bird has called to her with plaintive cries; his bad mother has passed by, singing and fluttering with a thousand airs and graces. Once only the father came near; he looked at his offspring with contempt, and then disappeared, never to return!

I crumbled some bread before the little orphan, but he did not know how to peck it with his bill. I tried to catch him, but he escaped into the forsaken nest. What will become of him there, if his mother does not come back!

August 15th, six o'clock. – This morning, on opening my window, I found the little bird dying upon the tiles; his wounds showed me that he had been driven from the nest by his unworthy mother. I tried in vain to warm him again with my breath; I felt the last pulsations of life; his eyes were already closed, and his wings hung down! I placed him on the roof in a ray of sunshine, and I closed my window. The struggle of life against death has always something gloomy in it: it is a warning to us.

Happily I hear someone in the passage; without doubt it is my old neighbor; his conversation will distract my thoughts.

It was my portress. Excellent woman! She wished me to read a letter from her son the sailor, and begged me to answer it for her.

I kept it, to copy it in my journal. Here it is:

"Dear Mother:

"This is to tell you that I have been very well ever since the last time, except that last week I was nearly drowned with the boat, which would have been a great loss, as there is not a better craft anywhere.

"A gust of wind capsized us; and just as I came up above water, I saw the captain sinking. I went after him, as was my duty, and, after diving three times, I brought him to the surface, which pleased him much; for when we were hoisted on board, and he had recovered his senses, he threw his arms round my neck, as he would have done to an officer.

"I do not hide from you, dear mother, that this has delighted me. But it isn't all; it seems that fishing up the captain has reminded them that I had a good character, and they have just told me that I am promoted to be a sailor of the first class! Directly I knew it, I cried out, 'My mother shall have coffee twice a day!' And really, dear mother, there is nothing now to hinder you, as I shall now have a larger allowance to send you.

"I include by begging you to take care of yourself if you wish to do me good; for nothing makes me feel so well as to think that you want for nothing.

"Your son, from the bottom of my heart,

"Jacques"

This is the answer that the portress dictated to me:

"My Good Jacquot:

"It makes me very happy to see that your heart is still as true as ever, and that you will never shame those who have brought you up. I need not tell you to take care of your life, because you know it is the same as my own, and that without you, dear child, I should wish for nothing but the grave; but we are not bound to live, while we are bound to do our duty.

"Do not fear for my health, good Jacques; I was never better! I do not grow old at all, for fear of making you unhappy. I want nothing, and I live like a lady. I even had some money over this year, and as my drawers shut very badly, I put it into the savings' bank, where I have opened an account in your name. So, when you come back, you will find yourself with an income. I have also furnished your chest with new linen, and I have knitted you three new sea-jackets.

"All your friends are well. Your cousin is just dead, leaving his widow in difficulties. I gave her your thirty francs' remittance and said that you had sent it her; and the poor woman remembers you day and night in her prayers. So, you see, I have put that money in another sort of savings' bank; but there it is our hearts that get the interest.

"Good-bye, dear Jacquot. Write to me often, and always remember the good God, and your old mother,

"PHROSINE MILLOT"

Good son, and worthy mother! how such examples bring us back to a love for the human race! In a fit of fanciful misanthropy, we may envy the fate of the savage, and prefer that of the bird to such as he; but impartial observation soon does justice to such paradoxes. We find, on examination, that in the mixed good and evil of human nature, the good so far abounds that we are not in the habit of noticing it, while the evil strikes us precisely on account of its being the exception. If nothing is perfect, nothing is so bad as to be without its compensation or its remedy. What spiritual riches are there in the midst of the evils of society! how much does the moral world redeem the material!

That which will ever distinguish man from the rest of creation, is his power of deliberate affection and of enduring self-sacrifice. The mother who took care of her brood in the corner of my window devoted to them the necessary time for accomplishing the laws which insure the preservation of her kind; but she obeyed an instinct, and not a rational choice. When she had accomplished the mission appointed her by Providence, she cast off the duty as we get rid of a burden, and she returned again to her selfish liberty. The other mother, on the contrary, will go on with her task as long as God shall leave her here below: the life of her son will still remain, so to speak, joined to her own; and when she disappears from the earth, she will leave there that part of herself.

Thus, the affections make for our species an existence separate from all the rest of creation. Thanks to them, we enjoy a sort of terrestrial immortality; and if other beings succeed one another, man alone perpetuates himself.

# Chapter IX

## THE FAMILY OF MICHAEL AROUT

September 15th, Eight O'clock

This morning, while I was arranging my books, Mother Genevieve came in, and brought me the basket of fruit I buy of her every Sunday. For the nearly twenty years that I have lived in this quarter, I have dealt in her little fruit-shop. Perhaps I should be better served elsewhere, but Mother Genevieve has but little custom; to leave her would do her harm, and cause her unnecessary pain. It seems to me that the length of our acquaintance has made me incur a sort of tacit obligation to her; my patronage has become her property.

She has put the basket upon my table, and as I want her husband, who is a joiner, to add some shelves to my bookcase, she has gone downstairs again immediately to send him to me.

At first I did not notice either her looks or the sound of her voice: but, now that I recall them, it seems to me that she was not as jovial as usual. Can Mother Genevieve be in trouble about anything?

Poor woman! All her best years were subject to such bitter trials, that she might think she had received her full share already. Were I to live a hundred years, I should never forget the circumstances which made her known to me, and which obtained for her my respect.

It was at the time of my first settling in the faubourg. I had noticed her empty fruit-shop, which nobody came into, and, being attracted by its forsaken appearance, I made my little purchases in it. I have always instinctively preferred the poor shops; there is less choice in them, but it seems to me that my purchase is a sign of sympathy with a brother in poverty. These little dealings are almost always an anchor of hope to those whose very existence is in peril – the only means by which some orphan gains a livelihood. There the aim of the tradesman is not to enrich himself, but to live! The purchase you make of him is more than an exchange – it is a good action.

Mother Genevieve at that time was still young, but had already lost that fresh bloom of youth which suffering causes to wither so soon among the poor. Her husband, a clever joiner, gradually left off working to become, according to the picturesque expression of the workshops, a worshipper of Saint Monday. The wages of the week, which was always reduced to two or three working days, were completely dedicated by him to the worship of this god of the Barriers,* and Genevieve was obliged herself to provide for all the wants of the household.

One evening, when I went to make some trifling purchases of her, I heard a sound of quarreling in the back shop. There were the voices of several women, among which I distinguished that of Genevieve, broken by sobs. On looking farther in, I perceived the fruit-woman holding a child in her arms, and kissing it, while a country nurse seemed to be claiming her wages from her. The poor woman, who without doubt had exhausted every explanation and every excuse, was crying in silence, and one of her neighbors was trying in vain to appease the countrywoman. Excited by that love of money which the evils of a hard peasant life but too well excuse, and disappointed by the refusal of her expected wages, the nurse was launching forth in recriminations, threats, and abuse. In spite of myself, I listened to the quarrel, not daring to interfere, and not thinking of going away, when Michael Arout appeared at the shop-door.

The joiner had just come from the Barriers, where he had passed part of the day at a public-house. His blouse, without a belt, and untied at the throat, showed none of the noble stains of work: in his hand he held his cap, which he had just picked up out of the mud; his hair was in disorder, his eye fixed, and the pallor of drunkenness in his face. He came reeling in, looked wildly around him, and called Genevieve.

She heard his voice, gave a start, and rushed into the shop; but at the sight of the miserable man, who was trying in vain to steady himself, she pressed the child in her arms, and bent over it with tears.

The countrywoman and the neighbor had followed her.

"Come! come!" cried the former in a rage, "do you intend to pay me, after all?"

"Ask the master for the money," ironically answered the woman from the next door, pointing to the joiner, who had just fallen against the counter.

The countrywoman looked at him.

"Ah! he is the father," returned she. "Well, what idle beggars! not to have a penny to pay honest people; and get tipsy with wine in that way."

The drunkard raised his head.

* The cheap wine shops are outside the Barriers, to avoid the octroi, or municipal excise.

"What! what!" stammered he; "who is it that talks of wine? I've had nothing but brandy! But I am going back again to get some wine! Wife, give me your money; there are some friends waiting for me at the *Père la Tuille.*"

Genevieve did not answer: he went round the counter, opened the till, and began to rummage in it.

"You see where the money of the house goes!" observed the neighbor to the countrywoman; "how can the poor unhappy woman pay you when he takes all?"

"Is that my fault?" replied the nurse, angrily. "They owe to me, and somehow or other they must pay me!"

And letting loose her tongue, as these women out of the country do, she began relating at length all the care she had taken of the child, and all the expense it had been to her. In proportion as she recalled all she had done, her words seemed to convince her more than ever of her rights, and to increase her anger. The poor mother, who no doubt feared that her violence would frighten the child, returned into the back shop, and put it into its cradle.

Whether it is that the countrywoman saw in this act a determination to escape her claims, or that she was blinded by passion, I cannot say; but she rushed into the next room, where I heard the sounds of quarreling, with which the cries of the child were soon mingled. The joiner, who was still rummaging in the till, was startled, and raised his head.

At the same moment Genevieve appeared at the door, holding in her arms the baby that the countrywoman was trying to tear from her. She ran toward the counter, and throwing herself behind her husband, cried:

"Michael, defend your son!"

The drunken man quickly stood up erect, like one who awakes with a start.

"My son!" stammered he; "what son?"

His looks fell upon the child; a vague ray of intelligence passed over his features.

"Robert," resumed he; "it is Robert!"

He tried to steady himself on his feet, that he might take the baby, but he tottered. The nurse approached him in a rage.

"My money, or I shall take the child away!" cried she. "It is I who have fed and brought it up: if you don't pay me for what has made it live, it ought to be the same to you as if it were dead. I shall not go until I have my due, or the baby."

"And what would you do with him?" murmured Genevieve, pressing Robert against her bosom.

"Take it to the Foundling!" replied the countrywoman, harshly; "the hospital is a better mother than you are, for it pays for the food of its little ones."

At the word "Foundling," Genevieve had exclaimed aloud in horror. With her arms wound round her son, whose head she hid in her bosom, and her two hands spread over him, she had retreated to the wall, and remained with her back against it, like a lioness defending her young. The neighbor and I contemplated this scene, without knowing how we could interfere. As for Michael, he looked at us by turns, making a visible effort to comprehend it all. When his eye rested upon Genevieve and the child, it lit up with a gleam of pleasure; but when he turned toward us, he again became stupid and hesitating.

At last, apparently making a prodigious effort, he cried out, "Wait!"

And going to a tub filled with water, he plunged his face into it several times.

Every eye was turned upon him; the countrywoman herself seemed astonished. At length he raised his dripping head. This ablution had partly dispelled his drunkenness; he looked at us for a moment, then he turned to Genevieve, and his face brightened up.

"Robert!" cried he, going up to the child, and taking him in his arms. "Ah! give him me, wife; I must look at him."

The mother seemed to give up his son to him with reluctance, and stayed before him with her arms extended, as if she feared the child would have a fall. The nurse began again in her turn to speak, and renewed her claims, this time threatening to appeal to law. At first Michael listened to her attentively, and when he comprehended her meaning, he gave the child back to its mother.

"How much do we owe you?" asked he.

The countrywoman began to reckon up the different expenses, which amounted to nearly thirty francs. The joiner felt to the bottom of his pockets, but could find nothing. His forehead became contracted by frowns; low curses began to escape him. All of a sudden he rummaged in his breast, drew forth a large watch, and holding it up above his head:

"Here it is – here's your money!" cried he with a joyful laugh; "a watch, a good one! I always said it would keep for a drink on a dry day; but it is not I who will drink it, but the young one. Ah! ah! ah! go and sell it for me, neighbor, and if that is not enough, I have my earrings. Eh! Genevieve, take them off for me; the earrings will square all! They shall not say you have been disgraced on account of the child – no, not even if I must pledge a bit of my flesh! My watch, my earrings, and my ring – get rid of all of them for me at the goldsmith's; pay the woman, and let the little fool go to sleep. Give him me, Genevieve; I will put him to bed."

And, taking the baby from the arms of his mother, he carried him with a firm step to his cradle.

It was easy to perceive the change which took place in Michael from this day. He cut all his old drinking acquaintances. He went early every morning to his work, and returned regularly in the evening to finish the day with Genevieve and Robert. Very soon he would not leave them at all, and he hired a place near the fruit-shop, and worked in it on his own account.

They would soon have been able to live in comfort, had it not been for the expenses which the child required. Everything was given up to his education. He had gone through the regular school training, had studied mathematics, drawing, and the carpenter's trade, and had only begun to work a few months ago. Till now, they had been exhausting every resource which their laborious industry could provide to push him forward in his business; and, happily, all these exertions had not proved useless: the seed had brought forth fruit, and the days of harvest were close by.

While I was thus recalling these remembrances to my mind, Michael had come in, and was occupied in fixing shelves where they were wanted.

During the time I was writing the notes of my journal, I was also scrutinizing the joiner.

The excesses of his youth and the labor of his manhood have deeply marked his face; his hair is thin and grey, his shoulders stoop, his legs are shrunken and slightly bent. There seems a sort of weight in his whole being. His very features have an expression of sorrow and despondency. He answers my questions by monosyllables, and like a man who wishes to avoid conversation. Whence comes this dejection, when one would think he had all he could wish for? I should like to know!

Ten o'clock. – Michael is just gone downstairs to look for a tool he has forgotten. I have at last succeeded in drawing from him the secret of his and Genevieve's sorrow. Their son Robert is the cause of it!

Not that he has turned out ill after all their care – not that he is idle or dissipated; but both were in hopes he would never leave them anymore. The presence of the young man was to have renewed and made glad their lives once more; his mother counted the days, his father prepared everything to receive their dear associate in their toils; and at the moment when they were thus about to be repaid for all their sacrifices, Robert had suddenly informed them that he had just engaged himself to a contractor at Versailles.

Every remonstrance and every prayer were useless; he brought forward the necessity of initiating himself into all the details of an important contract, the facilities he should have in his new position of improving himself in his trade, and the hopes he had of turning his knowledge to advantage. At, last, when his mother, having come to the end of her arguments, began to cry, he hastily kissed her, and went away that he might avoid any further remonstrances.

He had been absent a year, and there was nothing to give them hopes of his return. His parents hardly saw him once a month, and then he only stayed a few moments with them.

"I have been punished where I had hoped to be rewarded," Michael said to me just now. "I had wished for a saving and industrious son, and God has given me an ambitious and avaricious one! I had always said to myself that when once he was grown up we should have him always with us, to recall our youth and to enliven our hearts. His mother was always thinking of getting him married, and having children again to care for. You know women always will busy themselves about others. As for me, I thought of him working near my bench, and singing his new songs; for he has learnt music, and is one of the best singers at the Orpheon.

"A dream, sir, truly! Directly the bird was fledged, he took to flight, and remembers neither father nor mother. Yesterday, for instance, was the day we expected him; he should have come to supper with us. No Robert today, either! He has had some plan to finish, or some bargain to arrange, and his old parents are put down last in the accounts, after the customers and the joiner's work. Ah! if I could have guessed how it would have turned out! Fool! to have sacrificed my likings and my money, for nearly twenty years, to the education of a thankless son! Was it for this I took the trouble to cure myself of drinking, to break with my friends, to become an example to the neighborhood? The jovial good fellow has made a goose of himself. Oh! if I had to begin again! No, no! you see women and children are our bane. They soften our hearts; they lead us a life of hope and affection; we pass a quarter of our lives in fostering the growth of a grain of corn which is to be everything to us in our old age, and when the harvest-time comes – good-night, the ear is empty!"

While he was speaking, Michael's voice became hoarse, his eyes fierce, and his lips quivered. I wished to answer him, but I could only think of commonplace consolations, and I remained silent. The joiner pretended he needed a tool, and left me.

Poor father! Ah! I know those moments of temptation when virtue has failed to reward us, and we regret having obeyed her! Who has not felt this weakness in hours of trial, and who has not uttered, at least once, the mournful exclamation of Brutus?

But if virtue is only a word, what is there then in life that is true and real? No, I will not believe that goodness is in vain! It does not always give the happiness we had hoped for, but it brings some other. In the world everything is ruled by order, and has its proper and necessary consequences, and virtue cannot be the sole exception to the general law. If it had been prejudicial to those who practiced it, experience would have avenged them; but experience has, on the contrary, made it more universal and more holy. We only accuse it of being a faithless debtor because we demand an immediate payment, and one apparent to our senses. We always consider life as a fairytale, in which every good action must be rewarded by a visible wonder. We do not accept as payment a peaceful conscience, self-content, or a good name among men – treasures that are more precious than any other, but the value of which we do not feel till after we have lost them!

Michael is come back, and has returned to his work. His son has not yet arrived.

By telling me of his hopes and his grievous disappointments, he became excited; he unceasingly went over again the same subject, always adding something to his griefs. He had just wound up his confidential discourse by speaking to me of a joiner's business which he had hoped to buy, and work to good account with Robert's help. The present owner had made a fortune by it, and, after thirty years of business, he was thinking of retiring to one of the ornamental cottages in the outskirts of the city, a usual retreat for the frugal and successful workingman. Michael had not indeed the two thousand francs which must be paid down; but perhaps he could have persuaded Master Benoit to wait. Robert's presence would have been a security for him, for the young man could not fail to insure the prosperity of a workshop; besides science and skill, he had the power of invention and bringing to perfection. His father had discovered among his drawings a new plan for a staircase, which had occupied his thoughts for a long time; and he even suspected him of having engaged himself to the Versailles contractor for the very purpose of executing it. The youth was tormented by this spirit of invention, which took possession of all his thoughts, and, while devoting his mind to study, he had no time to listen to his feelings.

Michael told me all this with a mixed feeling of pride and vexation. I saw he was proud of the son he was abusing, and that his very pride made him more sensitive to that son's neglect.

Six o'clock P.M. – I have just finished a happy day. How many events have happened within a few hours, and what a change for Genevieve and Michael!

He had just finished fixing the shelves, and telling me of his son, while I laid the cloth for my breakfast.

Suddenly we heard hurried steps in the passage, the door opened, and Genevieve entered with Robert.

The joiner gave a start of joyful surprise, but he repressed it immediately, as if he wished to keep up the appearance of displeasure.

The young man did not appear to notice it, but threw himself into his arms in an open-hearted manner, which surprised me. Genevieve, whose face shone with happiness, seemed to wish to speak, and to restrain herself with difficulty.

I told Robert I was glad to see him, and he answered me with ease and civility.

"I expected you yesterday," said Michael Arout, rather dryly.

"Forgive me, father," replied the young workman, "but I had business at St. Germain's. I was not able to come back till it was very late, and then the master kept me."

The joiner looked at his son sidewise, and then took up his hammer again.

"All right," muttered he, in a grumbling tone; "when we are with other people we must do as they wish; but there are some who would like better to eat brown bread with their own knife than partridges with the silver fork of a master."

"And I am one of those, father," replied Robert, merrily, "but, as the proverb says, 'you must shell the peas before you can eat them.' It was necessary that I should first work in a great workshop –"

"To go on with your plan of the staircase," interrupted Michael, ironically.

"You must now say Monsieur Raymond's plan, father," replied Robert, smiling.

"Why?"

"Because I have sold it to him."

The joiner, who was planing a board, turned round quickly.

"Sold it!" cried he, with sparkling eyes.

"For the reason that I was not rich enough to give it him."

Michael threw down the board and tool.

"There he is again!" resumed he, angrily; "his good genius puts an idea into his head which would have made him known, and he goes and sells it to a rich man, who will take the honor of it himself."

"Well, what harm is there done?" asked Genevieve.

"What harm!" cried the joiner, in a passion. "You understand nothing about it – you are a woman; but he – he knows well that a true workman never gives up his own inventions for money, no more than a soldier would give up his cross. That is his glory; he is bound to keep it for the honor it does him! Ah, thunder! if I had ever made a discovery, rather than put it up at auction I would have sold one of my eyes! Don't you see that a new invention is like a child to a workman? He takes care of it, he brings it up, he makes a way for it in the world, and it is only a poor creature who sells it."

Robert colored a little.

"You will think differently, father," said he, "when you know why I sold my plan."

"Yes, and you will thank him for it," added Genevieve, who could no longer keep silence.

"Never!" replied Michael.

"But, wretched man!" cried she, "he sold it only for our sakes!"

The joiner looked at his wife and son with astonishment. It was necessary to come to an explanation. The latter related how he had entered into a negotiation with Master Benoit, who had positively refused to sell his business unless one half of the two thousand francs were first paid down. It was in the hopes of obtaining this sum that he had gone to work with the contractor at Versailles; he had had an opportunity of trying his invention, and of finding a purchaser. Thanks to the money he received for it, he had just concluded the bargain with Benoit, and had brought his father the key of the new work-yard.

This explanation was given by the young workman with so much modesty and simplicity that I was quite affected by it. Genevieve cried; Michael pressed his son to his heart, and in a long embrace he seemed to ask his pardon for having unjustly accused him.

All was now explained with honor to Robert. The conduct which his parents had ascribed to indifference really sprang from affection; he had neither obeyed the voice of ambition nor of avarice, nor even the nobler inspiration of inventive genius: his whole motive and single aim had been the happiness of Genevieve and Michael. The day for proving his gratitude had come, and he had returned them sacrifice for sacrifice!

After the explanations and exclamations of joy were over, all three were about to leave me; but, the cloth being laid, I added three more places, and kept them to breakfast.

The meal was prolonged: the fare was only tolerable; but the overflowings of affection made it delicious. Never had I better understood the unspeakable charm of family love. What calm enjoyment in that happiness which is always shared with others; in that community of interests which unites such various feelings; in that association of existences which forms one single being of so many! What is man without those home affections, which, like so many roots, fix him firmly in the earth, and permit him to imbibe all the juices of life? Energy, happiness – do not all these come from them? Without family life where would man learn to love, to associate, to deny himself? A community in little, is it not this which teaches us how to live in the great one? Such is the holiness of home, that, to express our relation with God, we have been obliged to borrow the words invented for our family life. Men have named themselves the sons of a heavenly Father!

Ah! let us carefully preserve these chains of domestic union. Do not let us unbind the human sheaf, and scatter its ears to all the caprices of chance and of the winds; but let us rather enlarge this holy law; let us carry the principles and the habits of home beyond set bounds; and, if it may be, let us realize the prayer of the Apostle of the Gentiles when he exclaimed to the newborn children of Christ: "Be ye like-minded, having the same love, being of one accord, of one mind."

# *Chapter X*

## OUR COUNTRY

October 12th, Seven O'clock A.M.

The nights are already become cold and long; the sun, shining through my curtains, no more wakens me long before the hour for work; and even when my eyes are open, the pleasant warmth of the bed keeps me fast under my counterpane. Every morning there begins a long argument between my activity and my indolence; and, snugly wrapped up to the eyes, I wait like the Gasçon, until they have succeeded in coming to an agreement.

This morning, however, a light, which shone from my door upon my pillow, awoke me earlier than usual. In vain I turned on my side; the persevering light, like a victorious enemy, pursued me into every position. At last, quite out of patience, I sat up and hurled my nightcap to the foot of the bed!

(I will observe, by way of parenthesis, that the various evolutions of this pacific headgear seem to have been, from the remotest time, symbols of the vehement emotions of the mind; for our language has borrowed its most common images from them.)

But be this as it may, I got up in a very bad humor, grumbling at my new neighbor, who took it into his head to be wakeful when I wished to sleep. We are all made thus; we do not understand that others may live on their own account. Each one of us is like the earth, according to the old system of Ptolemy, and thinks he can have the whole universe revolve around himself. On this point, to make use of the metaphor alluded to: *Tous les hommes ont la tête dans le meme bonnet.*

I had for the time being, as I have already said, thrown mine to the other end of my bed; and I slowly disengaged my legs from the warm bedclothes, while making a host of evil reflections upon the inconvenience of having neighbors.

For more than a month I had not had to complain of those whom chance had given me; most of them only came in to sleep, and went away again on rising. I was almost always alone on this top story – alone with the clouds and the sparrows!

But at Paris nothing lasts; the current of life carries us along, like the seaweed torn from the rock; the houses are vessels which take mere passengers. How many different faces have I already seen pass along the landing-place belonging to our attics! How many companions of a few days have disappeared forever! Some are lost in that medley of the living which whirls continually under the scourge of necessity, and others in that resting-place of the dead, who sleep under the hand of God!

Peter the bookbinder is one of these last. Wrapped up in selfishness, he lived alone and friendless, and he died as he had lived. His loss was neither mourned by anyone, nor disarranged anything in the world; there was merely a ditch filled up in the graveyard, and an attic emptied in our house.

It is the same which my new neighbor has inhabited for the last few days.

To say truly (now that I am quite awake, and my ill humor is gone with my nightcap) – to say truly, this new neighbor, although rising earlier than suits my idleness, is not the less a very good man: he carries his misfortunes, as few know how to carry their good fortunes, with cheerfulness and moderation.

But fate has cruelly tried him. Father Chaufour is but the wreck of a man. In the place of one of his arms hangs an empty sleeve; his left leg is made by the turner, and he drags the right along with difficulty; but above these ruins rises a calm and happy face. While looking upon his countenance, radiant with a serene energy, while listening to his voice, the tone of which has, so to speak, the accent of goodness, we see that the soul has remained entire in the half-destroyed covering. The fortress is a little damaged, as Father Chaufour says, but the garrison is quite hearty.

Decidedly, the more I think of this excellent man, the more I reproach myself for the sort of malediction I bestowed on him when I awoke.

We are generally too indulgent in our secret wrongs toward our neighbor. All ill-will which does not pass the region of thought seems innocent to us, and, with our clumsy justice, we excuse without examination the sin which does not betray itself by action!

But are we then bound to others only by the enforcement of laws? Besides these external relations, is there not a real relation of feeling between men? Do we not owe to all those who live under the same heaven as ourselves the aid not only of our acts but of our purposes? Ought not every human life to be to us like a vessel that we accompany with our prayers for a happy voyage? It is not enough that men do not harm one another; they must also help and love one another! The papal benediction, *Urbi et orbi!* should be the constant cry from all hearts. To condemn him who does not deserve it, even in the mind, even by a passing thought, is to break the great law, that which has established the union of souls here below, and to which Christ has given the sweet name of charity.

These thoughts came into my mind as I finished dressing, and I said to myself that Father Chaufour had a right to reparation from me. To make amends for the feeling of ill-will I had against him just now, I owed him some explicit proof of sympathy. I heard him humming a tune in his room; he was at work, and I determined that I would make the first neighborly call.

Eight o'clock P.M. – I found Father Chaufour at a table lighted by a little smoky lamp, without a fire, although it is already cold, and making large pasteboard boxes; he was humming a popular song in a low tone. I had hardly entered the room when he uttered an exclamation of surprise and pleasure.

"Eh! is it you, neighbor? Come in, then! I did not think you got up so early, so I put a damper on my music; I was afraid of waking you."

Excellent man! while I was sending him to the devil he was putting himself out of his way for me!

This thought touched me, and I paid my compliments on his having become my neighbor with a warmth which opened his heart.

"Faith! you seem to me to have the look of a good Christian," said he in a voice of soldierlike cordiality, and shaking me by the hand. "I do not like those people who look on a landing-place as a frontier line, and treat their neighbors as if they were Cossacks. When men snuff the same air, and speak the same lingo, they are not meant to turn their backs to each other. Sit down there, neighbor; I don't mean to order you; only take care of the stool; it has but three legs, and we must put good-will in place of the fourth."

"It seems that that is a treasure which there is no want of here," I observed.

"Good-will!" repeated Chaufour; "that is all my mother left me, and I take it no son has received a better inheritance. Therefore they used to call me Monsieur Content in the batteries."

"You are a soldier, then?"

"I served in the Third Artillery under the Republic, and afterward in the Guard, through all the commotions. I was at Jemappes and at Waterloo; so I was at the christening and at the burial of our glory, as one may say!"

I looked at him with astonishment.

"And how old were you then, at Jemappes?" asked I.

"Somewhere about fifteen," said he.

"How came you to think of being a soldier so early?"

"I did not really think about it. I then worked at toy-making, and never dreamed that France would ask me for anything else than to make her draft-boards, shuttlecocks, and cups and balls. But I had an old uncle at Vincennes whom I went to see from time to time – a Fontenoy veteran in the same rank of life as myself, but with ability enough to have risen to that of a marshal. Unluckily, in those days there was no way for common people to get on. My uncle, whose services would have got him made a prince under the other, had then retired with the mere rank of sub-lieutenant. But you should have seen him in his uniform, his cross of St. Louis, his wooden leg, his white moustaches, and his noble countenance. You would have said he was a portrait of one of those old heroes in powdered hair which are at Versailles!

"Every time I visited him, he said something which remained fixed in my memory. But one day I found him quite grave.

"'Jerome,' said he, 'do you know what is going on on the frontier?'

"'No, lieutenant,' replied I.

"'Well,' resumed he, 'our country is in danger!'

"I did not well understand him, and yet it seemed something to me.

"'Perhaps you have never thought what your country means,' continued he, placing his hand on my shoulder; 'it is all that surrounds you, all that has brought you up and fed you, all that you have loved! This ground that you see, these houses, these trees, those girls who go along there laughing – this is your country! The laws which protect you, the bread which pays for your work, the words you interchange with others, the joy and grief which come to you from the men and things among which you live – this is your country! The little room where you used to see your mother, the remembrances she has left you, the earth where she rests – this is your country! You see it, you breathe it, everywhere! Think to yourself, my son, of your rights and your duties, your affections and your wants, your past and your present blessings; write them all under a single name – and that name will be your country!'

"I was trembling with emotion, and great tears were in my eyes.

"'Ah! I understand,' cried I; 'it is our home in large; it is that part of the world where God has placed our body and our soul.'

"'You are right, Jerome,' continued the old soldier; 'so you comprehend also what we owe it.'

"'Truly,' resumed I, 'we owe it all that we are; it is a question of love.'

"'And of honesty, my son,' concluded he. 'The member of a family who does not contribute his share of work and of happiness fails in his duty, and is a bad kinsman; the member of a partnership who does not enrich it with all his might, with all his courage, and with all his heart, defrauds it of what belongs to it, and is a dishonest man. It is the same with him who enjoys the advantages of having a country, and does not accept the burdens of it; he forfeits his honor, and is a bad citizen!'

"'And what must one do, lieutenant, to be a good citizen?' asked I.

"'Do for your country what you would do for your father and mother,' said he.

"I did not answer at the moment; my heart was swelling, and the blood boiling in my veins; but on returning along the road, my uncle's words were, so to speak, written up before my eyes. I repeated, 'Do for your country what you would do for your father and mother.' And my country is in danger; an enemy attacks it, while I – I turn cups and balls!

"This thought tormented me so much all night that the next day I returned to Vincennes to announce to the lieutenant that I had just enlisted, and was going off to the frontier. The brave man pressed upon me his cross of St. Louis, and I went away as proud as an ambassador.

"That is how, neighbor, I became a volunteer under the Republic before I had cut my wisdom teeth."

All this was told quietly, and in the cheerful spirit of him who looks upon an accomplished duty neither as a merit nor a grievance.

While he spoke, Father Chaufour grew animated, not on account of himself, but of the general subject. Evidently that which occupied him in the drama of life was not his own part, but the drama itself.

This sort of disinterestedness touched me. I prolonged my visit, and showed myself as frank as possible, in order to win his confidence in return. In an hour's time he knew my position and my habits; I was on the footing of an old acquaintance.

I even confessed the ill-humor the light of his lamp put me into a short time before. He took what I said with the touching cheerfulness which comes from a heart in the right place, and which looks upon everything on the good side. He neither spoke to me of the necessity which obliged him to work while I could sleep, nor of the deprivations of the old soldier compared to the luxury of the young clerk; he only struck his forehead, accused himself of thoughtlessness, and promised to put list round his door!

O great and beautiful soul! with whom nothing turns to bitterness, and who art peremptory only in duty and benevolence!

October 15th. – This morning I was looking at a little engraving I had framed myself, and hung over my writing-table; it is a design of Gavarni's; in which, in a grave mood, he has represented a veteran and a conscript.

By often contemplating these two figures, so different in expression, and so true to life, both have become living in my eyes; I have seen them move, I have heard them speak; the picture has become a real scene, at which I am present as spectator.

The veteran advances slowly, his hand leaning on the shoulder of the young soldier. His eyes, closed forever, no longer perceive the sun shining through the flowering chestnut trees. In the place of his right arm hangs an empty sleeve, and he walks with a wooden leg, the sound of which on the pavement makes those who pass turn to look.

At the sight of this ancient wreck from our patriotic wars, the greater number shake their heads in pity, and I seem to hear a sigh or an imprecation.

"See the worth of glory!" says a portly merchant, turning away his eyes in horror.

"What a deplorable use of human life!" rejoins a young man who carries a volume of philosophy under his arm.

"The trooper would better not have left his plow," adds a countryman, with a cunning air.

"Poor old man!" murmurs a woman, almost crying.

The veteran has heard, and he knits his brow; for it seems to him that his guide has grown thoughtful. The latter, attracted by what he hears around him, hardly answers the old man's questions, and his eyes, vaguely lost in space, seem to be seeking there for the solution of some problem.

I seem to see a twitching in the grey moustaches of the veteran; he stops abruptly, and, holding back his guide with his remaining arm:

"They all pity me," says he, "because they do not understand it; but if I were to answer them –"

"What would you say to them, father?" asks the young man, with curiosity.

"I should say first to the woman who weeps when she looks at me, to keep her tears for other misfortunes; for each of my wounds calls to mind some struggle for my colors. There is room for doubting how some men have done their duty; with me it is visible. I carry the account of my services, written with the enemy's steel and lead, on myself; to pity me for having done my duty is to suppose I would better have been false to it."

"And what would you say to the countryman, father?"

"I should tell him that, to drive the plow in peace, we must first secure the country itself; and that, as long as there are foreigners ready to eat our harvest, there must be arms to defend it."

"But the young student, too, shook his head when he lamented such a use of life."

"Because he does not know what self-sacrifice and suffering can teach. The books that he studies we have put in practice, though we never read them: the principles he applauds we have defended with powder and bayonet."

"And at the price of your limbs and your blood. The merchant said, when he saw your maimed body, 'See the worth of glory!'"

"Do not believe him, my son: the true glory is the bread of the soul; it is this which nourishes self-sacrifice, patience, and courage. The Master of all has bestowed it as a tie the more between men. When we desire to be distinguished by our brethren, do we not thus prove our esteem and our sympathy for them? The longing for admiration is but one side of love. No, no; the true glory can never be too dearly paid for! That which we should deplore, child, is not the infirmities which prove a generous self-sacrifice, but those which our vices or our imprudence have called forth. Ah! if I could speak aloud to those who, when passing, cast looks of pity upon me, I should say to the young man whose excesses have dimmed his sight before he is old, 'What have you done with your eyes?' To the slothful man, who with difficulty drags along his enervated mass of flesh, 'What have you done with your feet?' To the old man, who is punished for his intemperance by the gout, 'What have you done with your hands?' To all, 'What have you done with the days God granted you, with the faculties you should have employed for the good of your brethren?' If you cannot answer, bestow no more of your pity upon the old soldier maimed in his country's cause; for he – he at least – can show his scars without shame."

October 16th. – The little engraving has made me comprehend better the merits of Father Chaufour, and I therefore esteem him all the more.

He has just now left my attic. There no longer passes a single day without his coming to work by my fire, or my going to sit and talk by his board.

The old artilleryman has seen much, and likes to tell of it. For twenty years he was an armed traveler throughout Europe, and he fought without hatred, for he was possessed by a single thought – the honor of the national flag! It might have been his superstition, if you will; but it was, at the same time, his safeguard.

The word FRANCE, which was then resounding so gloriously through the world, served as a talisman to him against all sorts of temptation. To have to support a great name may seem a burden to vulgar minds, but it is an encouragement to vigorous ones.

"I, too, have had many moments," said he to me the other day, "when I have been tempted to make friends with the devil. War is not precisely the school for rural virtues. By dint of burning, destroying, and killing, you grow a little tough as regards your feelings; and, when the bayonet has made you king, the notions of an autocrat come into your head a little strongly. But at these moments I called to mind that country which the lieutenant spoke of to me, and I whispered to myself the well-known phrase, *Toujours Français!* It has been laughed at since. People who would make a joke of the death of their mother have turned it into ridicule, as if the name of our country was not also a noble and a binding thing. For my part, I shall never forget from how many follies the title of Frenchman has kept me. When, overcome with fatigue, I have found myself in the rear of the colors, and when the musketry was rattling in the front ranks, many a time I heard a voice, which whispered in my ear, 'Leave the others to fight, and for today take care of your own hide!' But then, that word Français! murmured within me, and I pressed forward to help my comrades. At other times, when, irritated by hunger, cold, and wounds, I have arrived at the hovel of some Meinherr, I have been seized by an itching to break the master's back, and to burn his hut; but I whispered to myself, Français! and this name would not rhyme with either incendiary or murderer. I have, in this way, passed through kingdoms from east to west, and from north to south, always determined not to bring disgrace upon my country's flag. The lieutenant, you see, had taught me a magic word – My country! Not only must we defend it, but we must also make it great and loved."

October 17th. – Today I have paid my neighbor a long visit. A chance expression led the way to his telling me more of himself than he had yet done.

I asked him whether both his limbs had been lost in the same battle.

"No, no!" replied he; "the cannon only took my leg; it was the Clamart quarries that my arm went to feed."

And when I asked him for the particulars –

"That's as easy as to say good-morning," continued he. "After the great break-up at Waterloo, I stayed three months in the camp hospital to give my wooden leg time to grow. As soon as I was able to hobble a little, I took leave of headquarters, and took the road to Paris, where I hoped to find some relative or friend; but no – all were gone, or underground. I should have found myself less strange at Vienna, Madrid, or Berlin. And although I had a leg the less to provide for, I was none the better off; my appetite had come back, and my last sous were taking flight.

"I had indeed met my old colonel, who recollected that I had helped him out of the skirmish at Montereau by giving him my horse, and he had offered me bed and board at his house. I knew that the year before he had married a castle and no few farms, so that I might become permanent coat-brusher to a millionaire, which was not without its temptations. It remained to see if I had not anything better to do. One evening I set myself to reflect upon it.

"'Let us see, Chaufour,' said I to myself; 'the question is to act like a man. The colonel's place suits you, but cannot you do anything better? Your body is still in good condition, and your arms strong; do you not owe all your strength to your country, as your Vincennes uncle said? Why not leave some old soldier, more cut up than you are, to get his hospital at the colonel's? Come, trooper, you are still fit for another stout charge or two! You must not lay up before your time.'

"Whereupon I went to thank the colonel, and to offer my services to an old artilleryman, who had gone back to his home at Clamart, and who had taken up the quarryman's pick again.

"For the first few months I played the conscript's part – that is to say, there was more stir than work; but with a good will one gets the better of stones, as of everything else. I did not become, so to speak, the leader of a column, but I brought up the rank among the good workmen, and I ate my bread with a good appetite, seeing I had earned it with a good will. For even underground, you see, I still kept my pride. The thought that I was working to do my part in changing rocks into houses pleased my heart. I said to myself, 'Courage, Chaufour, my old boy; you are helping to beautify your country.' And that kept up my spirit.

"Unfortunately, some of my companions were rather too sensible to the charms of the brandy-bottle; so much so, that one day one of them, who could hardly distinguish his right hand from his left, thought proper to strike a light close to a charged mine. The mine exploded suddenly, and sent a shower of stone grape among us, which killed three men, and carried away the arm of which I have now only the sleeve."

"So you were again without means of living?" said I to the old soldier.

"That is to say, I had to change them," replied he, quietly. "The difficulty was to find one which would do with five fingers instead of ten; I found it, however."

"How was that?"

"Among the Paris street-sweepers."

"What! you have been one –"

"Of the pioneers of the health force for a while, neighbor, and that was not my worst time either. The corps of sweepers is not so low as it is dirty, I can tell you! There are old actresses in it who could never learn to save their money, and ruined merchants from the exchange; we even had a professor of classics, who for a little drink would recite Latin to you, or Greek tragedies, as you chose. They could not have competed for the Monthyon prize; but we excused faults on account of poverty, and cheered our poverty by our good-humor and jokes. I was as ragged and as cheerful as the rest, while trying to be something better. Even in the mire of the gutter I preserved my faith that nothing is dishonorable which is useful to our country.

"'Chaufour,' said I to myself with a smile, 'after the sword, the hammer; after the hammer, the broom; you are going downstairs, my old boy, but you are still serving your country.'"

"'However, you ended by leaving your new profession?' said I."

"A reform was required, neighbor. The street-sweepers seldom have their feet dry, and the damp at last made the wounds in my good leg open again. I could no longer follow the regiment, and it was necessary to lay down my arms. It is now two months since I left off working in the sanitary department of Paris.

"At the first moment I was daunted. Of my four limbs, I had now only my right hand, and even that had lost its strength; so it was necessary to find some gentlemanly occupation for it. After trying a little of everything, I fell upon card-box making, and here I am at cases for the lace and buttons of the national guard; it is work of little profit, but it is within the capacity of all. By getting up at four and working till eight, I earn sixty-five centimes; my lodging and bowl of soup take fifty of them, and there are three sous over for luxuries. So I am richer than France herself, for I have no deficit in my budget; and I continue to serve her, as I save her lace and buttons."

At these words Father Chaufour looked at me with a smile, and with his great scissors began cutting the green paper again for his cardboard cases. My heart was touched, and I remained lost in thought.

Here is still another member of that sacred phalanx who, in the battle of life, always march in front for the example and the salvation of the world! Each of these brave soldiers has his war-cry; for this one it is "Country," for that "Home," for a third "Mankind;" but they all follow the same standard – that of duty; for all the same divine law reigns – that of self-sacrifice. To love something more than one's self – that is the secret of all that is great; to know how to live for others – that is the aim of all noble souls.

# *Chapter XI*

## MORAL USE OF INVENTORIES

November 13th, Nine O'clock P.M.

I had well stopped up the chinks of my window; my little carpet was nailed down in its place; my lamp, provided with its shade, cast a subdued light around, and my stove made a low, murmuring sound, as if some live creature was sharing my hearth with me.

All was silent around me. But, out of doors the snow and rain swept the roofs, and with a low, rushing sound ran along the gurgling gutters; sometimes a gust of wind forced itself beneath the tiles, which rattled together like castanets, and afterward it was lost in the empty corridor. Then a slight and pleasurable shiver thrilled through my veins: I drew the flaps of my old wadded dressing gown around me, I pulled my threadbare velvet cap over my eyes, and, letting myself sink deeper into my easy chair, while my feet basked in the heat and light which shone through the door of the stove, I gave myself up to a sensation of enjoyment, made more lively by the consciousness of the storm which raged without. My eyes, swimming in a sort of mist, wandered over all the details of my peaceful abode; they passed from my prints to my bookcase, resting upon the little chintz sofa, the white curtains of the iron bedstead, and the portfolio of loose papers – those archives of the attics; and then, returning to the book I held in my hand, they attempted to seize once more the thread of the reading which had been thus interrupted.

In fact, this book, the subject of which had at first interested me, had become painful to me. I had come to the conclusion that the pictures of the writer were too somber. His description of the miseries of the world appeared exaggerated to me; I could not believe in such excess of poverty and of suffering; neither God nor man could show themselves so harsh toward the sons of Adam. The author had yielded to an artistic temptation: he was making a show of the sufferings of humanity, as Nero burned Rome for the sake of the picturesque.

Taken altogether, this poor human house, so often repaired, so much criticized, is still a pretty good abode; we may find enough in it to satisfy our wants, if we know how to set bounds to them; the happiness of the wise man costs but little, and asks but little space.

These consoling reflections became more and more confused. At last my book fell on the ground without my having the resolution to stoop and take it up again; and insensibly overcome by the luxury of the silence, the subdued light, and the warmth, I fell asleep.

I remained for some time lost in the sort of insensibility belonging to a first sleep; at last some vague and broken sensations came over me. It seemed to me that the day grew darker, that the air became colder. I half perceived bushes covered with the scarlet berries which foretell the coming of winter. I walked on a dreary road, bordered here and there with juniper trees white with frost. Then the scene suddenly changed. I was in the diligence; the cold wind shook the doors and windows; the trees, loaded with snow, passed by like ghosts; in vain I thrust my benumbed feet into the crushed straw. At last the carriage stopped, and, by one of those stage effects so common in sleep, I found myself alone in a barn, without a fireplace, and open to the winds on all sides. I saw again my mother's gentle face, known only to me in my early childhood, the noble and stern countenance of my father, the little fair head of my sister, who was taken from us at ten years old; all my dead family lived again around me; they were there, exposed to the bitings of the cold and to the pangs of hunger. My mother prayed by the resigned old man, and my sister, rolled up on some rags of which they had made her a bed, wept in silence, and held her naked feet in her little blue hands.

It was a page from the book I had just read transferred into my own existence.

My heart was oppressed with inexpressible anguish. Crouched in a corner, with my eyes fixed upon this dismal picture, I felt the cold slowly creeping upon me, and I said to myself with bitterness:

"Let us die, since poverty is a dungeon guarded by suspicion, apathy, and contempt, and from which it is vain to try to escape; let us die, since there is no place for us at the banquet of the living!"

And I tried to rise to join my mother again, and to wait at her feet for the hour of release.

This effort dispelled my dream, and I awoke with a start.

I looked around me; my lamp was expiring, the fire in my stove extinguished, and my half-opened door was letting in an icy wind. I got up, with a shiver, to shut and double-lock it; then I made for the alcove, and went to bed in haste.

But the cold kept me awake a long time, and my thoughts continued the interrupted dream.

The pictures I had lately accused of exaggeration now seemed but a too faithful representation of reality; and I went to sleep without being able to recover my optimism – or my warmth.

Thus did a cold stove and a badly closed door alter my point of view. All went well when my blood circulated properly; all looked gloomy when the cold laid hold on me.

This reminds me of the story of the duchess who was obliged to pay a visit to the neighboring convent on a winter's day. The convent was poor, there was no wood, and the monks had nothing but their discipline and the ardor of their prayers to keep out the cold. The duchess, who was shivering with cold, returned home, greatly pitying the poor monks. While the servants were taking off her cloak and adding two more logs to her fire, she called her steward, whom she ordered to send some wood to the convent immediately. She then had her couch moved close to the fireside, the warmth of which soon revived her. The recollection of what she had just suffered was speedily lost in her present comfort, when the steward came in again to ask how many loads of wood he was to send.

"Oh! you may wait," said the great lady carelessly; "the weather is very much milder."

Thus, man's judgments are formed less from reason than from sensation; and as sensation comes to him from the outward world, so he finds himself more or less under its influence; by little and little he imbibes a portion of his habits and feelings from it.

It is not, then, without cause that, when we wish to judge of a stranger beforehand, we look for indications of his character in the circumstances which surround him. The things among which we live are necessarily made to take our image, and we unconsciously leave in them a thousand impressions of our minds. As we can judge by an empty bed of the height and attitude of him who has slept in it, so the abode of every man discovers to a close observer the extent of his intelligence and the feelings of his heart. Bernardin de St.-Pierre has related the story of a young girl who refused a suitor because he would never have flowers or domestic animals in his house. Perhaps the sentence was severe, but not without reason. We may presume that a man insensible to beauty and to humble affection must be ill prepared to feel the enjoyments of a happy marriage.

14th, seven o'clock P.M. – This morning, as I was opening my journal to write, I had a visit from our old cashier.

His sight is not so good as it was, his hand begins to shake, and the work he was able to do formerly is now becoming somewhat laborious to him. I had undertaken to write out some of his papers, and he came for those I had finished.

We conversed a long time by the stove, while he was drinking a cup of coffee which I made him take.

M. Rateau is a sensible man, who has observed much and speaks little; so that he has always something to say.

While looking over the accounts I had prepared for him, his look fell upon my journal, and I was obliged to acknowledge that in this way I wrote a diary of my actions and thoughts every evening for private use. From one thing to another, I began speaking to him of my dream the day before, and my reflections about the influence of outward objects upon our ordinary sentiments. He smiled.

"Ah! you, too, have my superstitions," he said, quietly. "I have always believed, like you, that you may know the game by the lair: it is only necessary to have tact and experience; but without them we commit ourselves to many rash judgments. For my part. I have been guilty of this more than once, but sometimes I have also drawn a right conclusion. I recollect especially an adventure which goes as far back as the first years of my youth –"

He stopped. I looked at him as if I waited for his story, and he told it me at once.

At this time he was still but third clerk to an attorney at Orleans. His master had sent him to Montargis on different affairs, and he intended to return in the diligence the same evening, after having received the amount of a bill at a neighboring town; but they kept him at the debtor's house, and when he was able to set out the day had already closed.

Fearing not to be able to reach Montargis in good time, he took a crossroad they pointed out to him. Unfortunately the fog increased, no star was visible in the heavens, and the darkness became so great that he lost his road. He tried to retrace his steps, passed twenty footpaths, and at last was completely astray.

After the vexation of losing his place in the diligence, came the feeling of uneasiness as to his situation. He was alone, on foot, lost in a forest, without any means of finding his right road again, and with a considerable sum of money about him, for which he was responsible. His anxiety was increased by his inexperience. The idea of a forest was connected in his mind with so many adventures of robbery and murder, that he expected some fatal encounter every instant.

To say the truth, his situation was not encouraging. The place was not considered safe, and for some time past there had been rumors of the sudden disappearance of several horse-dealers, though there was no trace of any crime having been committed.

Our young traveler, with his eyes staring forward, and his ears listening, followed a footpath which he supposed might take him to some house or road; but woods always succeeded to woods. At last he perceived a light at a distance, and in a quarter of an hour he reached the highroad.

A single house, the light from which had attracted him, appeared at a little distance. He was going toward the entrance gate of the courtyard, when the trot of a horse made him turn his head. A man on horseback had just appeared at the turning of the road, and in an instant was close to him.

The first words he addressed to the young man showed him to be the farmer himself. He related how he had lost himself, and learned from the countryman that he was on the road to Pithiviers. Montargis was three leagues behind him.

The fog had insensibly changed into a drizzling rain, which was beginning to wet the young clerk through; he seemed afraid of the distance he had still to go, and the horseman, who saw his hesitation, invited him to come into the farmhouse.

It had something of the look of a fortress. Surrounded by a pretty high wall, it could not be seen except through the bars of the great gate, which was carefully closed. The farmer, who had got off his horse, did not go near it, but, turning to the right, reached another entrance closed in the same way, but of which he had the key.

Hardly had he passed the threshold when a terrible barking resounded from each end of the yard. The farmer told his guest to fear nothing, and showed him the dogs chained up to their kennels; both were of an extraordinary size, and so savage that the sight of their master himself could not quiet them.

A boy, attracted by their barking, came out of the house and took the farmer's horse. The latter began questioning him about some orders he had given before he left the house, and went toward the stable to see that they had been executed.

Thus left alone, our clerk looked about him.

A lantern which the boy had placed on the ground cast a dim light over the courtyard. All around seemed empty and deserted. Not a trace was visible of the disorder often seen in a country farmyard, and which shows a temporary cessation of the work which is soon to be resumed again. Neither a cart forgotten where the horses had been unharnessed, nor sheaves of corn heaped up ready for threshing, nor a plow overturned in a corner and half hidden under the freshly-cut clover. The yard was swept, the barns shut up and padlocked. Not a single vine creeping up the walls; everywhere stone, wood, and iron!

He took up the lantern and went up to the corner of the house. Behind was a second yard, where he heard the barking of a third dog, and a covered wall was built in the middle of it.

Our traveler looked in vain for the little farm garden, where pumpkins of different sorts creep along the ground, or where the bees from the hives hum under the hedges of honeysuckle and elder. Verdure and flowers were nowhere to be seen. He did not even perceive the sight of a poultry-yard or pigeon-house. The habitation of his host was everywhere wanting in that which makes the grace and the life of the country.

The young man thought that his host must be of a very careless or a very calculating disposition, to concede so little to domestic enjoyments and the pleasures of the eye; and judging, in spite of himself, by what he saw, he could not help feeling a distrust of his character.

In the meantime the farmer returned from the stables, and made him enter the house.

The inside of the farmhouse corresponded to its outside. The whitewashed walls had no other ornament than a row of guns of all sizes; the massive furniture hardly redeemed its clumsy appearance by its great solidity. The cleanliness was doubtful, and the absence of all minor conveniences proved that a woman's care was wanting in the household concerns. The young clerk learned that the farmer, in fact, lived here with no one but his two sons.

Of this, indeed, the signs were plain enough. A table with the cloth laid, that no one had taken the trouble to clear away, was left near the window. The plates and dishes were scattered upon it without any order, and loaded with potato-parings and half-picked bones. Several empty bottles emitted an odor of brandy, mixed with the pungent smell of tobacco smoke.

After seating his guest, the farmer lighted his pipe, and his two sons resumed their work by the fireside. Now and then the silence was just broken by a short remark, answered by a word or an exclamation; and then all became as mute as before.

"From my childhood," said the old cashier, "I had been very sensible to the impression of outward objects; later in life, reflection had taught me to study the causes of these impressions rather than to drive them away. I set myself, then, to examine everything around me with great attention.

"Below the guns, I had remarked on entering, some wolftraps were suspended, and to one of them still hung the mangled remains of a wolf's paw, which they had not yet taken off from the iron teeth. The blackened chimneypiece was ornamented by an owl and a raven nailed on the wall, their wings extended, and their throats with a huge nail through each; a fox's skin, freshly flayed, was spread before the window; and a larder hook, fixed into the principal beam, held a headless goose, whose body swayed about over our heads.

"My eyes were offended by all these details, and I turned them again upon my hosts. The father, who sat opposite to me, only interrupted his smoking to pour out his drink, or address some reprimand to his sons. The eldest of these was scraping a deep bucket, and the bloody scrapings, which he threw into the fire every instant, filled the room with a disagreeable fetid smell; the second son was sharpening some butcher's knives. I learned from a word dropped from the father that they were preparing to kill a pig the next day.

"These occupations and the whole aspect of things inside the house told of such habitual coarseness in their way of living as seemed to explain, while it formed the fitting counterpart of, the forbidding gloominess of the outside. My astonishment by degrees changed into disgust, and my disgust into uneasiness. I cannot detail the whole chain of ideas which succeeded one another in my imagination; but, yielding to an impulse I could not overcome, I got up, declaring I would go on my road again.

"The farmer made some effort to keep me; he spoke of the rain, of the darkness, and of the length of the way. I replied to all by the absolute necessity there was for my being at Montargis that very night; and thanking him for his brief hospitality, I set off again in a haste which might well have confirmed the truth of my words to him.

"However, the freshness of the night and the exercise of walking did not fail to change the directions of my thoughts. When away from the objects which had awakened such lively disgust in me, I felt it gradually diminishing. I began to smile at the susceptibility of my feelings, and then, in proportion as the rain became heavier and colder, these strictures on myself assumed a tone of ill-temper. I silently accused myself of the absurdity of mistaking sensation for admonitions of my reason. After all, were not the farmer and his sons free to live alone, to hunt, to keep dogs, and to kill a pig? Where was the crime of it? With less nervous susceptibility, I should have accepted the shelter they offered me, and I should now be sleeping snugly on a truss of straw, instead of walking with difficulty through the cold and drizzling rain. I thus continued to reproach myself, until, toward morning, I arrived at Montargis, jaded and benumbed with cold.

"When, however, I got up refreshed, toward the middle of the next day, I instinctively returned to my first opinion. The appearance of the farmhouse presented itself to me under the same repulsive colors which the evening before had determined me to make my escape from it. Reason itself remained silent when reviewing all those coarse details, and was forced to recognize in them the indications of a low nature, or else the presence of some baleful influence.

"I went away the next day without being able to learn anything concerning the farmer or his sons; but the recollection of my adventure remained deeply fixed in my memory.

"Ten years afterward I was traveling in the diligence through the department of the Loiret; I was leaning from the window, and looking at some coppice ground now for the first time brought under cultivation, and the mode of clearing which one of my traveling companions was explaining to me, when my eyes fell upon a walled enclosure, with an iron-barred gate. Inside it I perceived a house with all the blinds closed, and which I immediately recollected; it was the farmhouse where I had been sheltered. I eagerly pointed it out to my companion, and asked who lived in it.

"'Nobody just now,' replied he.

"'But was it not kept, some years ago, by a farmer and his two sons?'

"'The Turreaus;' said my traveling companion, looking at me; 'did you know them?'

"'I saw them once.'

"He shook his head.

"'Yes, yes!' resumed he; 'for many years they lived there like wolves in their den; they merely knew how to till land, kill game, and drink. The father managed the house, but men living alone, without women to love them, without children to soften them, and without God to make them think of heaven, always turn into wild beasts, you see; so one morning the eldest son, who had been drinking too much brandy, would not harness the plow-horses; his father struck him with his whip, and the son, who was mad drunk, shot him dead with his gun.'"

16th, P.M. – I have been thinking of the story of the old cashier these two days; it came so opportunely upon the reflections my dream had suggested to me.

Have I not an important lesson to learn from all this?

If our sensations have an incontestable influence upon our judgments, how comes it that we are so little careful of those things which awaken or modify these sensations? The external world is always reflected in us as in a mirror, and fills our minds with pictures which, unconsciously to ourselves, become the germs of our opinions and of our rules of conduct. All the objects which surround us are then, in reality, so many talismans whence good and evil influences are emitted, and it is for us to choose them wisely, so as to create a healthy atmosphere for our minds.

Feeling convinced of this truth, I set about making a survey of my attic.

The first object on which my eyes rest is an old map of the history of the principal monastery in my native province. I had unrolled it with much satisfaction, and placed it on the most conspicuous part of the wall. Why had I given it this place? Ought this sheet of old worm-eaten parchment to be of so much value to me, who am neither an antiquary nor a scholar? Is not its real importance in my sight that one of the abbots who founded it bore my name, and that I shall, perchance, be able to make myself a genealogical tree of it for the edification of my visitors? While writing this, I feel my own blushes. Come, down with the map! let us banish it into my deepest drawer.

As I passed my glass, I perceived several visiting cards complacently displayed in the frame. By what chance is it that there are only names that make a show among them? Here is a Polish count – a retired colonel – the deputy of my department. Quick, quick, into the fire with these proofs of vanity! and let us put this card in the handwriting of our office-boy, this direction for cheap dinners, and the receipt of the broker where I bought my last armchair, in their place. These indications of my poverty will serve, as Montaigne says, *mater ma superbe,* and will always make me recollect the modesty in which the dignity of the lowly consists.

I have stopped before the prints hanging upon the wall. This large and smiling Pomona, seated on sheaves of corn, and whose basket is overflowing with fruit, only produces thoughts of joy and plenty; I was looking at her the other day, when I fell asleep denying such a thing as misery. Let us give her as companion this picture of Winter, in which everything tells of sorrow and suffering: one picture will modify the other.

And this Happy Family of Greuze's! What joy in the children's eyes! What sweet repose in the young woman's face! What religious feeling in the grandfather's countenance! May God preserve their happiness to them! but let us hang by its side the picture of this mother, who weeps over an empty cradle. Human life has two faces, both of which we must dare to contemplate in their turn.

Let me hide, too, these ridiculous monsters which ornament my chimneypiece. Plato has said that "the beautiful is nothing else than the visible form of the good." If it is so, the ugly should be the visible form of the evil, and, by constantly beholding it, the mind insensibly deteriorates.

But above all, in order to cherish the feelings of kindness and pity, let me hang at the foot of my bed this affecting picture of the Last Sleep! Never have I been able to look at it without feeling my heart touched.

An old woman, clothed in rags, is lying by a roadside; her stick is at her feet, and her head rests upon a stone; she has fallen asleep; her hands are clasped; murmuring a prayer of her childhood, she sleeps her last sleep, she dreams her last dream!

She sees herself, again a strong and happy child, keeping the sheep on the common, gathering the berries from the hedges, singing, curtsying to passers-by, and making the sign of the cross when the first star appears in the heavens! Happy time, filled with fragrance and sunshine! She wants nothing yet, for she is ignorant of what there is to wish for.

But see her grown up; the time is come for working bravely: she must cut the corn, thresh the wheat, carry the bundles of flowering clover or branches of withered leaves to the farm. If her toil is hard, hope shines like a sun over everything and it wipes the drops of sweat away. The growing girl already sees that life is a task, but she still sings as she fulfills it.

By-and-bye the burden becomes heavier; she is a wife, she is a mother! She must economize the bread of today, have her eye upon the morrow, take care of the sick, and sustain the feeble; she must act, in short, that part of an earthly Providence, so easy when God gives us his aid, so hard when he forsakes us. She is still strong, but she is anxious; she sings no longer!

Yet a few years, and all is overcast. The husband's health is broken; his wife sees him pine away by the now fireless hearth; cold and hunger finish what sickness had begun; he dies, and his widow sits on the ground by the coffin provided by the charity of others, pressing her two half-naked little ones in her arms. She dreads the future, she weeps, and she droops her head.

At last the future has come; the children are grown up, but they are no longer with her. Her son is fighting under his country's flag, and his sister is gone. Both have been lost to her for a long time – perhaps forever; and the strong girl, the brave wife, the courageous mother, is henceforth only a poor old beggar-woman, without a family, and without a home! She weeps no more, sorrow has subdued her; she surrenders, and waits for death.

Death, that faithful friend of the wretched, is come: not hideous and with mockery, as superstition represents, but beautiful, smiling, and crowned with stars! The gentle phantom stoops to the beggar; its pale lips murmur a few airy words, which announce to her the end of her labors; a peaceful joy comes over the aged beggarwoman, and, leaning on the shoulder of the great Deliverer, she has passed unconsciously from her last earthly sleep to her eternal rest.

Lie there, thou poor way-wearied woman! The leaves will serve thee for a winding-sheet. Night will shed her tears of dew over thee, and the birds will sing sweetly by thy remains. Thy visit here below will not have left more trace than their flight through the air; thy name is already forgotten, and the only legacy thou hast to leave is the hawthorn stick lying forgotten at thy feet!

Well! someone will take it up – some soldier of that great human host which is scattered abroad by misery or by vice; for thou art not an exception, thou art an instance; and under the same sun which shines so pleasantly upon all, in the midst of these flowering vineyards, this ripe corn, and these wealthy cities, entire generations suffer, succeed each other, and still bequeath to each the beggar's stick!

The sight of this sad picture shall make me more grateful for what God has given me, and more compassionate for those whom he has treated with less indulgence; it shall be a lesson and a subject for reflection for me.

Ah! if we would watch for everything that might improve and instruct us; if the arrangements of our daily life were so disposed as to be a constant school for our minds! but oftenest we take no heed of them. Man is an eternal mystery to himself; his own person is a house into which he never enters, and of which he studies the outside alone. Each of us need have continually before him the famous inscription which once instructed Socrates, and which was engraved on the walls of Delphi by an unknown hand:

KNOW THYSELF

# Chapter XII

## THE END OF THE YEAR

December 30th, P.M.

I was in bed, and hardly recovered from the delirious fever which had kept me for so long between life and death. My weakened brain was making efforts to recover its activity; my thoughts, like rays of light struggling through the clouds, were still confused and imperfect; at times I felt a return of the dizziness which made a chaos of all my ideas, and I floated, so to speak, between alternate fits of mental wandering and consciousness.

Sometimes everything seemed plain to me, like the prospect which, from the top of some high mountain, opens before us in clear weather. We distinguish water, woods, villages, cattle, even the cottage perched on the edge of the ravine; then suddenly there comes a gust of wind laden with mist, and all is confused and indistinct.

Thus, yielding to the oscillations of a half-recovered reason, I allowed my mind to follow its various impulses without troubling myself to separate the real from the imaginary; I glided softly from one to the other, and my dreams and waking thoughts succeeded closely upon one another.

Now, while my mind is wandering in this unsettled state, see, underneath the clock which measures the hours with its loud ticking, a female figure appears before me!

At first sight I saw enough to satisfy me that she was not a daughter of Eve. In her eye was the last flash of an expiring star, and her face had the pallor of an heroic death-struggle. She was dressed in a drapery of a thousand changing colors of the brightest and the most somber hues, and held a withered garland in her hand.

After having contemplated her for some moments, I asked her name, and what brought her into my attic. Her eyes, which were following the movements of the clock, turned toward me, and she replied:

"You see in me the year which is just drawing to its end; I come to receive your thanks and your farewell."

I raised myself on my elbow in surprise, which soon gave place to bitter resentment.

"Ah! you want thanks," cried I; "but first let me know what for?

"When I welcomed your coming, I was still young and vigorous: you have taken from me each day some little of my strength, and you have ended by inflicting an illness upon me; already, thanks to you, my blood is less warm, my muscles less firm, and my feet less agile than before! You have planted the germs of infirmity in my bosom; there, where the summer flowers of life were growing, you have wickedly sown the nettles of old age!

"And, as if it were not enough to weaken my body, you have also diminished the powers of my soul; you have extinguished her enthusiasm; she is become more sluggish and more timid. Formerly her eyes took in the whole of mankind in their generous survey; but you have made her nearsighted, and now she hardly sees beyond herself! That is what you have done for my spiritual being: then as to my outward existence, see to what grief, neglect, and misery you have reduced it! For the many days that the fever has kept me chained to this bed, who has taken care of this home in which I placed all my joy? Shall I not find my closets empty, my bookcase, stripped, all my poor treasures lost through negligence or dishonesty? Where are the plants I cultivated, the birds I fed? All are gone! my attic is despoiled, silent and solitary! As it is only for the last few moments that I have returned to a consciousness of what surrounds me, I am even ignorant who has nursed me during my long illness! Doubtless some hireling, who will leave when all my means of recompense are exhausted! And what will my masters, for whom I am bound to work, have said to my absence? At this time of the year, when business is most pressing, can they have done without me, will they even have tried to do so? Perhaps I am already superseded in the humble situation by which I earned my daily bread! And it is thou-thou alone, wicked daughter of Time – who hast brought all these misfortunes upon me: strength, health, comfort, work – thou hast taken all from me. I have only received outrage and loss from thee, and yet thou darest to claim my gratitude!"

"Ah! die then, since thy day is come; but die despised and cursed; and may I write on thy tomb the epitaph the Arabian poet inscribed upon that of a king:

"'*Rejoice, thou passer-by: he whom we have buried here cannot live again.*'"

I was wakened by a hand taking mine; and opening my eyes, I recognized the doctor.

After having felt my pulse, he nodded his head, sat down at the foot of the bed, and looked at me, rubbing his nose with his snuffbox. I have since learned that this was a sign of satisfaction with the doctor.

"Well! so we wanted old snub-nose to carry us off?" said M. Lambert, in his half-joking, half-scolding way. "What the deuce of a hurry we were in! It was necessary to hold you back with both arms at least!"

"Then you had given me up, doctor?" asked I, rather alarmed.

"Not at all," replied the old physician. "We can't give up what we have not got; and I make it a rule never to have any hope. We are but instruments in the hands of Providence, and each of us should say, with Ambroise Pare: 'I tend him, God cures him!'"

"May He be blessed then, as well as you," cried I; "and may my health come back with the new year!"

M. Lambert shrugged his shoulders.

"Begin by asking yourself for it," resumed he, bluntly. "God has given it you, and it is your own sense, and not chance, that must keep it for you. One would think, to hear people talk, that sickness comes upon us like the rain or the sunshine, without one having a word to say in the matter. Before we complain of being ill we should prove that we deserve to be well."

I was about to smile, but the doctor looked angry.

"Ah! you think that I am joking," resumed he, raising his voice; "but tell me, then, which of us gives his health the same attention that he gives to his business? Do you economize your strength as you economize your money? Do you avoid excess and imprudence in the one case with the same care as extravagance or foolish speculations in the other? Do you keep as regular accounts of your mode of living as you do of your income? Do you consider every evening what has been wholesome or unwholesome for you, with the same care that you bring to the examination of your expenditure? You may smile; but have you not brought this illness on yourself by a thousand indiscretions?"

I began to protest against this, and asked him to point out these indiscretions. The old doctor spread out his fingers, and began to reckon upon them one by one.

"Primo," cried he, "want of exercise. You live here like a mouse in a cheese, without air, motion, or change. Consequently, the blood circulates badly, the fluids thicken, the muscles, being inactive, do not claim their share of nutrition, the stomach flags, and the brain grows weary.

"Secundo. Irregular food. Caprice is your cook; your stomach a slave who must accept what you give it, but who presently takes a sullen revenge, like all slaves.

"Tertio. Sitting up late. Instead of using the night for sleep, you spend it in reading; your bedstead is a bookcase, your pillows a desk! At the time when the wearied brain asks for rest, you lead it through these nocturnal orgies, and you are surprised to find it the worse for them the next day.

"Quarto. Luxurious habits. Shut up in your attic, you insensibly surround yourself with a thousand effeminate indulgences. You must have list for your door, a blind for your window, a carpet for your feet, an easy chair stuffed with wool for your back, your fire lit at the first sign of cold, and a shade to your lamp; and thanks to all these precautions, the least draft makes you catch cold, common chairs give you no rest, and you must wear spectacles to support the light of day. You have thought you were acquiring comforts, and you have only contracted infirmities.

"Quinto"

"Ah! enough, enough, doctor!" cried I. "Pray, do not carry your examination farther; do not attach a sense of remorse to each of my pleasures."

The old doctor rubbed his nose with his snuffbox.

"You see," said he, more gently, and rising at the same time, "you would escape from the truth. You shrink from inquiry – a proof that you are guilty. *Habemus confitentem reum!* But at least, my friend, do not go on laying the blame on Time, like an old woman."

Thereupon he again felt my pulse, and took his leave, declaring that his function was at an end, and that the rest depended upon myself.

When the doctor was gone, I set about reflecting upon what he had said.

Although his words were too sweeping, they were not the less true in the main. How often we accuse chance of an illness, the origin of which we should seek in ourselves! Perhaps it would have been wiser to let him finish the examination he had begun.

But is there not another of more importance – that which concerns the health of the soul? Am I so sure of having neglected no means of preserving that during the year which is now ending? Have I, as one of God's soldiers upon earth, kept my courage and my arms efficient? Shall I be ready for the great review of souls which must pass before Him WHO IS in the dark valley of Jehoshaphat?

Darest thou examine thyself, O my soul! and see how often thou hast erred?

First, thou hast erred through pride! for I have not duly valued the lowly. I have drunk too deeply of the intoxicating wines of genius, and have found no relish in pure water. I have disdained those words which had no other beauty than their sincerity; I have ceased to love men solely because they are men – I have loved them for their endowments; I have contracted the world within the narrow compass of a pantheon, and my sympathy has been awakened by admiration only. The vulgar crowd, which I ought to have followed with a friendly eye because it is composed of my brothers in hope or grief, I have let pass by with as much indifference as if it were a flock of sheep. I am indignant with him who rolls in riches and despises the man poor in worldly wealth; and yet, vain of my trifling knowledge, I despise him who is poor in mind – I scorn the poverty of intellect as others do that of dress; I take credit for a gift which I did not bestow on myself, and turn the favor of fortune into a weapon with which to attack others.

Ah! if, in the worst days of revolutions, ignorance has revolted and raised a cry of hatred against genius, the fault is not alone in the envious malice of ignorance, but comes in part, too, from the contemptuous pride of knowledge.

Alas! I have too completely forgotten the fable of the two sons of the magician of Baghdad.

One of them, struck by an irrevocable decree of destiny, was born blind, while the other enjoyed all the delights of sight. The latter, proud of his own advantages, laughed at his brother's blindness, and disdained him as a companion. One morning the blind boy wished to go out with him.

"To what purpose," said he, "since the gods have put nothing in common between us? For me creation is a stage, where a thousand charming scenes and wonderful actors appear in succession; for you it is only an obscure abyss, at the bottom of which you hear the confused murmur of an invisible world. Continue then alone in your darkness, and leave the pleasures of light to those upon whom the day-star shines."

With these words he went away, and his brother, left alone, began to cry bitterly. His father, who heard him, immediately ran to him, and tried to console him by promising to give him whatever he desired.

"Can you give me sight?" asked the child.

"Fate does not permit it," said the magician.

"Then," cried the blind boy, eagerly, "I ask you to put out the sun!"

Who knows whether my pride has not provoked the same wish on the part of someone of my brothers who does not see?

But how much oftener have I erred through levity and want of thought! How many resolutions have I taken at random! how many judgments have I pronounced for the sake of a witticism! how many mischiefs have I not done without any sense of my responsibility! The greater part of men harm one another for the sake of doing something. We laugh at the honor of one, and compromise the reputation of another, like an idle man who saunters along a hedgerow, breaking the young branches and destroying the most beautiful flowers.

And, nevertheless, it is by this very thoughtlessness that the fame of some men is created. It rises gradually, like one of those mysterious mounds in barbarous countries, to which a stone is added by every passerby; each one brings something at random, and adds it as he passes, without being able himself to see whether he is raising a pedestal or a gibbet. Who will dare look behind him, to see his rash judgments held up there to view?

Some time ago I was walking along the edge of the green mound on which the Montmartre telegraph stands. Below me, along one of the zigzag paths which wind up the hill, a man and a girl were coming up, and arrested my attention. The man wore a shaggy coat, which gave him some resemblance to a wild beast; and he held a thick stick in his hand, with which he described various strange figures in the air. He spoke very loud, and in a voice which seemed to me convulsed with passion. He raised his eyes every now and then with an expression of savage harshness, and it appeared to me that he was reproaching and threatening the girl, and that she was listening to him with a submissiveness which touched my heart. Two or three times she ventured a few words, doubtless in the attempt to justify herself; but the man in the greatcoat began again immediately with his loud and angry voice, his savage looks, and his threatening evolutions in the air. I followed him with my eyes, vainly endeavoring to catch a word as he passed, until he disappeared behind the hill.

I had evidently just seen one of those domestic tyrants whose sullen tempers are excited by the patience of their victims, and who, though they have the power to become the beneficent gods of a family, choose rather to be their tormentors.

I cursed the unknown savage in my heart, and I felt indignant that these crimes against the sacred peace of home could not be punished as they deserve, when I heard his voice approaching nearer. He had turned the path, and soon appeared before me at the top of the slope.

The first glance, and his first words, explained everything to me: in place of what I had taken for the furious tones and terrible looks of an angry man, and the attitude of a frightened victim, I had before me only an honest citizen, who squinted and stuttered, but who was explaining the management of silkworms to his attentive daughter.

I turned homeward, smiling at my mistake; but before I reached my faubourg I saw a crowd running, I heard calls for help, and every finger pointed in the same direction to a distant column of flame. A manufactory had taken fire, and everybody was rushing forward to assist in extinguishing it.

I hesitated. Night was coming on; I felt tired; a favorite book was awaiting me; I thought there would be no want of help, and I went on my way.

Just before I had erred from want of consideration; now it was from selfishness and cowardice.

But what! have I not on a thousand other occasions forgotten the duties which bind us to our fellowmen? Is this the first time I have avoided paying society what I owe it? Have I not always behaved to my companions with injustice, and like the lion? Have I not claimed successively every share? If anyone is so ill-advised as to ask me to return some little portion, I get provoked, I am angry, I try to escape from it by every means. How many times, when I have perceived a beggar sitting huddled up at the end of the street, have I not gone out of my way, for fear that compassion would impoverish me by forcing me to be charitable! How often have I doubted the misfortunes of others, that I might with justice harden my heart against them.

With what satisfaction have I sometimes verified the vices of the poor man, in order to show that his misery is the punishment he deserves!

Oh! let us not go farther – let us not go farther! I interrupted the doctor's examination, but how much sadder is this one! We pity the diseases of the body; we shudder at those of the soul.

I was happily disturbed in my reverie by my neighbor, the old soldier.

Now I think of it, I seem always to have seen, during my fever, the figure of this good old man, sometimes leaning against my bed, and sometimes sitting at his table, surrounded by his sheets of pasteboard.

He has just come in with his glue-pot, his quire of green paper, and his great scissors. I called him by his name; he uttered a joyful exclamation, and came near me.

"Well! so the bullet is found again!" cried he, taking my two hands into the maimed one which was left him; "it has not been without trouble, I can tell you; the campaign has been long enough to win two clasps in. I have seen no few fellows with the fever batter windmills during my hospital days: at Leipzig, I had a neighbor who fancied a chimney was on fire in his stomach, and who was always calling for the fire-engines; but the third day it all went out of itself. But with you it has lasted twenty-eight days – as long as one of the Little Corporal's campaigns."

"I am not mistaken then; you were near me?"

"Well! I had only to cross the passage. This left hand has not made you a bad nurse for want of the right; but, bah! you did not know what hand gave you drink, and it did not prevent that beggar of a fever from being drowned – for all the world like Poniatowski in the Elster."

The old soldier began to laugh, and I, feeling too much affected to speak, pressed his hand against my breast. He saw my emotion, and hastened to put an end to it.

"By-the-bye, you know that from today you have a right to draw your rations again," resumed he gaily; "four meals, like the German meinherrs – nothing more! The doctor is your house steward."

"We must find the cook, too," replied I, with a smile.

"She is found," said the veteran.

"Who is she?"

"Genevieve."

"The fruit-woman?"

"While I am talking she is cooking for you, neighbor; and do not fear her sparing either butter or trouble. As long as life and death were fighting for you, the honest woman passed her time in going up and down stairs to learn which way the battle went. And, stay, I am sure this is she."

In fact we heard steps in the passage, and he went to open the door.

"Oh, well!" continued he, "it is Mother Millot, our portress, another of your good friends, neighbor, and whose poultices I recommend to you. Come in, Mother Millot – come in; we are quite bonny boys this morning, and ready to step a minuet if we had our dancing-shoes."

The portress came in, quite delighted. She brought my linen, washed and mended by herself, with a little bottle of Spanish wine, the gift of her sailor son, and kept for great occasions. I would have thanked her, but the good woman imposed silence upon me, under the pretext that the doctor had forbidden me to speak. I saw her arrange everything in my drawers, the neat appearance of which struck me; an attentive hand had evidently been there, and day by day put straight the unavoidable disorder consequent on sickness.

As she finished, Genevieve arrived with my dinner; she was followed by Mother Denis, the milk-woman over the way, who had learned, at the same time, the danger I had been in, and that I was now beginning to be convalescent. The good Savoyard brought me a new-laid egg, which she herself wished to see me eat.

It was necessary to relate minutely all my illness to her. At every detail she uttered loud exclamations; then, when the portress warned her to be less noisy, she excused herself in a whisper. They made a circle around me to see me eat my dinner; each mouthful I took was accompanied by their expressions of satisfaction and thankfulness. Never had the King of France, when he dined in public, excited such admiration among the spectators.

As they were taking the dinner away, my colleague, the old cashier, entered in his turn.

I could not prevent my heart beating as I recognized him. How would the heads of the firm look upon my absence, and what did he come to tell me?

I waited with inexpressible anxiety for him to speak; but he sat down by me, took my hand, and began rejoicing over my recovery, without saying a word about our masters. I could not endure this uncertainty any longer.

"And the Messieurs Durmer," asked I, hesitatingly, "how have they taken – the interruption to my work?"

"There has been no interruption," replied the old clerk, quietly.

"What do you mean?"

"Each one in the office took a share of your duty; all has gone on as usual, and the Messieurs Durmer have perceived no difference."

This was too much. After so many instances of affection, this filled up the measure. I could not restrain my tears.

Thus the few services I had been able to do for others had been acknowledged by them a hundredfold! I had sown a little seed, and every grain had fallen on good ground, and brought forth a whole sheaf. Ah! this completes the lesson the doctor gave me. If it is true that the diseases, whether of the mind or body, are the fruit of our follies and our vices, sympathy and affection are also the rewards of our having done our duty. Everyone of us, with God's help, and within the narrow limits of human capability, himself makes his own disposition, character, and permanent condition.

Everybody is gone; the old soldier has brought me back my flowers and my birds, and they are my only companions. The setting sun reddens my half-closed curtains with its last rays. My brain is clear, and my heart lighter. A thin mist floats before my eyes, and I feel myself in that happy state which precedes a refreshing sleep.

Yonder, opposite the bed, the pale goddess in her drapery of a thousand changing colors, and with her withered garland, again appears before me; but this time I hold out my hand to her with a grateful smile.

"Adieu, beloved year! whom I but now unjustly accused. That which I have suffered must not be laid to thee; for thou wast but a tract through which God had marked out my road – a ground where I had reaped the harvest I had sown. I will love thee, thou wayside shelter, for those hours of happiness thou hast seen me enjoy; I will love thee even for the suffering thou hast seen me endure. Neither happiness nor suffering came from thee; but thou hast been the scene for them. Descend again then, in peace, into eternity, and be blest, thou who hast left me experience in the place of youth, sweet memories instead of past time, and gratitude as payment for good offices."

www.ingramcontent.com/pod-product-compliance
Lightning Source LLC
Chambersburg PA
CBHW030419310726
48979CB00007B/1108
*9781603128889*